calves in the mud room

Jerome O Brown

Calves in the Mud Room

By Jerome O Brown

Copyright © 2013 Jerome O Brown

Title font by Billy Argel

Print book design by 52 Novels

Cover design and photography by Jerome O Brown

This is a work of fiction. Names, characters, places, brands, media, and incidents are either the product of the author's imagination or are used fictitiously. Any resemblance to similarly named places or to persons living or deceased is unintentional.

ISBN: 978-0615967509

For Mel, Leta, Bud, Shirl, and Sharon

My gratitude to all the invisible hands and big medicine in my life.

Fellow writers Jim Anderson and Ken Bennett for their insights and inspiration.

Rebecca Faith Heyman for her editing and counsel.

Dave and Jean for being who they are.

My friends and teachers.

And for the spill of their light and joy, my pretty girl and our family.

CALVES IN THE MUD ROOM

one

Visions of Glory Schoonover — head cheerleader, honor student, student council secretary, Spud Festival Princess; her juicy fruit lips, dark chocolate eyes, honey-streaked corn silk hair with the chamomile-lavender scent; the thick, erotic syrup of her Emeraude perfume; the outline of the wispy, white lace peek-a-boob bra beneath the flimsy cream top with the pearl buttons; the way her round, rubbery breasts rise and fall with each breath; the sling of the slinky, burning-pink thong panties clinging to the soft band of baby fat that rides the low-cut, hip-hugging, crotch-squirming, tight-ass-affirming jeans — all disappear, vanish the instant the truck lights sweep through the pin streaks of snow and gunmetal fog and land on the smoky blobs of rump roast, rib eyes, t-bones, tenderloins, flank strips, hot dogs and moo-burger piling up at the gate and blocking Wade Summers' way.

Stupid cows. Stand in cow shit all day cows.

God, he hates cattle.

They're waiting to be fed. They're always waiting to be fed. All the light bred out them. All the efficiencies injected into them. His grandfather never did it that way. No protein supplements, antibiotics, growth hormones or corn. He was old school and rejected chemical farming. Take care of the animals first, he would say, and they'll take care of you.

God, he misses his grandfather.

The gate screeches as he pushes it into the herd. The chain clanks against cold metal. The cows snort, stumble and bellow in retreat.

He watches so none blunder out before he can drive through, close it back up, then slog through the red clay mush to the house.

It's barely four and already as dark as six. The mountain, fat snowflakes, and dense ground-hugging fog blot out the low-arcing sun of late winter.

So where's the Buick? His mom's car. She said he could use it for tonight's date.

• • •

Why Glory Schoonover asked him to the Valentine's Day Sponge Dance, he could not fathom. It was too good to be true. They had never spoken. Not really. Twice in Contemporary World Problems she had caught him staring at her. Both times she smiled that smile. The one that gives boys pleasure and the girls power.

Wade was so shocked and swirling in disbelief, excitement, elation, unworthiness, and suspicion of a joke being played, of being punked, of not being enough, that he almost blurted no. But it was her, Glory Schoonover in person, in a yellow tank top and sassy jeans, not a text or email, standing there in front of his locker right before American History, asking him to the tolo. So instead he blurted why.

"Why? Why not?" Glory asked.

"I don't know."

"You don't know why not, or you don't know if you'll go with me?"

"I'm sorry, I didn't mean to say that. I'm so stupid, I know, yes, thank you, yes."

"Well, you can't be stupid any more. You'll be with me."

Glory pecked him on the cheek and spun away, the kiss and her smell euphoric.

"Glory?" Boy, saying that sounded good. "There is something you should probably know. I've never been to a dance."

"That makes it even better. I'll be your first."

• • •

The wind whips the TV antenna and sucks the door shut behind him. The manufactured home shudders and creaks.

A frozen chicken, still in the plastic wrapper, sits in a pink puddle in the kitchen sink.

"Where's mom?"

"The cable and internet's off again," his little brother answers.

"Are you going to fix us dinner?" Dot asks.

Neither one looks up from their PlayStation.

"Where is she?"

"Doreen's," his brother says, as if there's any other option.

Wade checks his phone. No bars, no tone, no surprise.

The landline still hums. He tries his mom's cell and gets the "this number is currently not available" recording. He finds Doreen's number below Runza's Pizza in the old metal address book.

His mom answers while Doreen slices the lime and stirs the mix for margarita Friday.

"Are you comin' home soon?"

"No."

"Should I come get the car?"

"What?"

"For the dance tonight."

"Oh that's right, sweet sixteen and never been kissed." She licks salt from the rim of her glass.

"Seventeen."

"It's a figure of speech. Your dad might let you use the Silverado since it's a special occasion."

"But you said."

"Things change, hon. It's either that or your grandfather's pickup.

"I can't take a date in that."

"Oh, it's not that bad. She won't mind. It's kind of cute actually. I saw a rig just like that in the Sundance catalog for $35,000."

"It probably didn't have a hole in the floorboard or a seat you couldn't sit on without a wire sprung up your butt."

"Don't go getting smart." She puts the glass down and stirs with her finger. "Talk to your dad. You never know. He did say he'd feed."

"He's not my dad."

"He provides."

"The cell, the cable, and internet are cut off again."

"I just sent those bastards a check."

"Will you talk to him for me?"

"Can't you do anything for yourself?"

Wade puts the phone back in its cradle.

"Mom said you'd fix us dinner," says Dot.

"Yeah, well, mom says a lot of things."

• • •

The snow blows sideways on the drive into town. Cars crawl, spin and slide.

"I can't wait for tonight," Glory had said just before Contemporary World Problems. "Don't be late. I don't want to miss anything." She stood so close he could see the blonde hairs on her cheek and smell the Tic Tac on her breath.

Late? Are you kidding? I'll be there early.

The black badass Silverado with the temporary license taped to the back window straddles two parking spots alongside the Collision Center. Wade's supposed stepdad, Dwain, works in the radiator shop.

Everywhere you look around the place is a sign: DANGER CAUSTIC lead work area; Yes, We're Open; Free Quotes; NO CHECKS; Repairing, Recoring, Cleaning; We plug leaks; Employees Only Beyond This Point; POISON No smoking or eating.

Sounds like a fun place. I always eat radiators and smoke anti-freeze.

"This better be good." Dwain lights up a smoke and begins cleaning his fingernails.

"Did mom talk to you?"

Dwain stays blank.

"She reneged on the Buick and I was wondering if you'd trade me rigs?" Wade holds up the keys.

"No."

"Please. I got a date."

"I don't know what to tell ya, rent a limo."

A limo? There aren't any limos around here. "You still gonna feed tonight?"

Dwain frowns.

"You told mom you would."

"I must have been drunk, real drunk." His stepdad puts away the clippers and rubs his hands with a red grease rag. "Don't ever come down here again and bother me at work."

Wade turns to go.

"And get this snow shoveled off the shop roof."

"There's not that much."

"Then it won't take long."

This was an overreaction to a freak storm they had last year just before Mother's Day when two feet of heavy slush landed. Wade and his granddad had just lifted the auger off the back of the tractor when the shop roof started to buckle.

While his granddad raised the bucket to support the main beam, Wade climbed onto the roof with a scoop shovel. The wet gooey snow glued itself to the shovel and each time Wade tried to heave it off, he almost went over the edge with it.

Try rakin' it, Dwain yelled before running inside the house.

The metal strips stretched, ripped and burped. The roof sagged some more and with a shrug, evicted Wade and the ladder like a horse twitching flies from its neck.

He hit the hard ground hard. Harder than getting bucked from a rodeo bronc.

His stepdad returned with the 12-gauge. Ducked inside and gut shot the roof.

The boy thought the man stunned stupid.

His grandfather, who months earlier had questioned the cheap stick construction, just walked away.

While Dwain jammed in some more shells for another go at it, the main beam continued to bow around the tractor bucket. More panels split at the seams. More screws unscrewed. Still the roof did not cave. Never fully collapsed. Just sort of bent over and vomited chunks of slush, slapping his stepdad and the shotgun to the concrete slab.

So now the man's paranoid about a little snow.

• • •

The back of the old truck hauls scattered stems of straw and alfalfa leaves, a scoop shovel (no handle), a pitchfork, a dented spray can of DW40, a rusty set of tire chains, a flattened box of windshield wipers, one battery cable (black), an empty red gas can (no cap), a wad of bent-up barb wire, miles of orange twine, a spool of electric fence wire, rubber irrigation boots, a run-over straw hat, an empty tub of horse vitamins, and one old fallen-down cowboy boot with the spur still riding the heel (left foot).

The cab looks like someone broke in and dumped an office desk drawer on the dashboard, then came back with a toolbox and emptied it on the floor.

Wade collects a bent screwdriver, an ice scraper, a heavy-duty metal cutter (you could cut a car open with this puppy), a socket set still in the red plastic holder, two Crescent wrenches (one about four inches long, the other about two feet), a hoof scraper, a flashlight (still works), an unopened can of Udder Balm, and one frozen flat glove (right hand, hole in thumb).

On the dash sits opened and unopened mail, bills and statements, a flier for a used hayin' package (cutter, baler and rake) marked down from 25 grand to 17; a cigar box full of paper clips, rubber bands, pens, pencils, two black sharpies and four silver dollars (minted in 1896); a box of horseshoe nails, a red Conoco Hottest Brand Going to-go cup, an empty staple gun, a pocket calendar from Barlow's Feed with appointments and the day's temperatures, and the calving log book for the last few years (#9919 eats rocks).

Wade follows the loops of the old man's handwriting with his finger.

On the gun rack hangs a crusty brown mustard Filson duster, a halter and lead, a coil of nylon rope, a crowbar, leather chaps, and the other spur. He examines the spur. It's a Crockett with heart, diamond, jack and spade inlays. His grandfather won them at Cheyenne Frontier Days in the 40's for calf ropin'.

What doesn't fit into one of the Hefty trash bags he found under the seat, he places off to the side, except for the spurs, duster, rope, and crowbar. Those he shoves under the seat. The Udder Balm, horseshoe nails and hoof cleaner he crams into the jockey box, on top of a thick manila envelope with The Metcalf Law Office stamped in the upper left corner.

Wade chips away at the frozen mud, manure, and straw on the floor with the ice scraper before running the rig through the carwash.

He splurges for The Works and that's just what he gets. Sudsy water with a bubble gum smell runs down the windows. Inside and out.

The more he tries to clean up inside the cab, the more of a mess he makes. The mixed media collage of farm dander just smears. He hits it with the power sprayer. Gets as much as he can. Water runs from the floorboards and out the doors. Now the seat is soggy and the engine dead.

He gets under the hood. Dries the battery cable connections, takes off the air cleaner, and runs a rag through the carburetor. Like any of that will work.

Yeah, just like the one in the Sundance catalog.

He pulls out the throttle and pushes the starter button.

Please, please, please God, please.

It turns and whirls with that old Ford whine. The charge's still strong; the spark catches.

Between this and Glory, Wade figures all of his prayers are up.

He loads the rest of the junk into the bed and steers the old pickup out of the Wash-O-Mat and past EZ Pawn, Bail Bonds, Tatts and Piercings. It used to be an Army/Navy recruiting office, which was open only one afternoon a week. A faded THE ONE, THE ONLY, THE MARINES poster still hangs in the window next to a dayglo banner screaming EL DOLAR SUPERIOR PARA EL ORO.

Wade wonders about all the bikes chained out front and who pawned them. The kids or the parents? He's pretty sure he knows the answer.

He lets the truck idle in front of Chet's Flowers. Next door is Medical Oxygen Respirator Sales (50% off green dot sale). Directly across the street is Professional Oxygen

Supply (UPS NO) and next to it is Bob Faw Pharmacy (Walkers and Wheelchairs 10% off).

A sandwich board on the corner lists: DIVORCE, WILLS, NOTARY, CHRISTIAN COUNSELING.

The flower shop is a cold, damp cave. Smells of mold and mildew. White latticework runs along the cinder block walls behind pedestals covered with artificial grass. The shelves are mostly empty, maybe due to the special on funeral arrangements. The flowers locked in the glass refrigerator have seen happier days.

Laura Stanky's mom works in her black ski parka, gray sweats, knit cap and knockoff Uggs. She talks into her cell phone, giving the listener a play by play — oh, it's just some high school kid who special ordered an orchid. Uh-huh. God only knows.

Wade peeks inside the wrapping at the delicate stem. He wanted Glory to have something special. Not just a mum or rose like everyone else. He wanted something unique and different. Something memorable. But this is not what he saw online.

"It won't bloom for another couple of days, hon, then it'll be real pretty." He couldn't tell if she was talking to him or into the phone.

Wade goes on faith.

Across the street the hard fluorescents give the drug store a surreal cast. The wheelchairs and walkers that are on sale crowd the entrance. Wade walks to the back where this kinda hippie girl sells candles, lotions and other organic type junk. Wade smells several bars of handcrafted soap several times before deciding on one from France with sage. He also gets a juniper-cypress bath and body oil, a new kind of organic shampoo, a tiny bottle of Binaca, and a tube of lip balm. You never know.

He stops under the Family Planning sign and studies a package of Ultra-Ribbed-ECSTASY-Feels-Like-Nothing's-There-Super-Comfort-Shape-Ultrasmooth-Lubricant Trojan Brand Latex Condoms.

Bob Faw himself looks down from the pharmacist's counter. Wade's courage and fantasy evaporate under the judgmental glare.

TWO

Six bales of alfalfa and a half bag of cake ride the tailgate out to the pasture. The cows bunch up into the corner of the fence, butts to the blowing snow.

Wade jams the tranny into granny gear and jumps out. The old Ford staggers over frozen cow pies and wheezes along the feed line. He snaps the orange twine and spreads the flakes.

A loner with a curled tail forsakes dinner. She lies down, gets back up, uneasy and restless. All the signs of calving and a month early. But who knew about this bunch Dwain added to his grandfather's herd of steady Angus?

Not tonight, no, not tonight, please.

He finishes feeding and swings the truck back around. The snow etches an opaque curtain and he loses the isolated heifer.

A black cow pie in the headlights sprouts a pair of legs and tries to rise. Wade hits the brake hard. The engine croaks.

Snowflakes eat at the newborn. There's no story of birth in the snow. No fluids, no hoof prints, no imprint. The mother could be twenty feet away but all he sees are shreds of snow.

Probably a first-time heifer. Some never know what to do. They'll just stand there, step on the baby, never mother up, even wander off.

He's sure this one hasn't suckled or been licked. The hind legs are frozen to the ground.

The crowbar becomes a precision tool in Wade's ham-sized fist. He gently pokes and pries the calf from the earth, easily scoops up the eighty pounds and settles it inside the cab. Their eyes meet.

"Yup, this is life. Welcome."

The old Ford fires back up without a prayer and crawls through the locust frenzy of flakes. Wade turns the heater up to high hissing and picks away the icy membrane and crusty mucus on the black and white face in his lap.

He can't tell for sure which direction he's going. His landmarks are gone. No fence line, no feed line, no herd, house, out buildings, corrals, neighbor lights, or horizon to guide him. It's all just white gauze.

He brakes, maybe best to wait it out. Wisps of black appear and disappear with each smear of the windshield wipers. It's the feed line. He gets his bearings and steers for the barn.

The headlights find the loner again. Wade inches the truck up to her rump.

Her bag's sprung.

A nose and feet stick out.

Wade clicks on the high beams. The calf has a purple tongue. Not a good sign. It's in distress. Probably not getting enough oxygen. If the umbilical cord is twisted, it's a goner.

He needs to get her on the jack and get the calf pulled right away.

He smashes his fist on the steering wheel. I do not need this shit. Not tonight. Of all the nights. Not tonight. You can freeze until you're a rock for all I care.

He gets a halter and rope on her, hitches her to the back bumper and tows her to the barn.

The calf in the cab should be fine as long as it stays warm and gets some colostrum within an hour. Its immune system needs the nutrients and antibodies the milk substitute provides.

It could take that long, even longer, to pull the other one. But if he can finish in an hour, he can get to Glory's on time.

Wade tries to fashion the frozen Filson into a blanket, but it's about as malleable as plywood. He pulls off his hoodie and wraps it around the baby Big Mac.

He sets the emergency brake, lets the heater whine and engine churn. No joy rides, he tells the black eyes.

Only one stall is open and accessible. A stack of 2-by-10s, a couple of chop saws, a toilet, boxes of bathroom fixtures, copper pipes and several huge rolls of insulation his stepdad's been collecting live in one. The snow machine and ATV fill up another, and Dwain hoards the keys. The old John Deere, an immoveable beast on a dead battery, blocks the other.

He ties the cow to a post and puts down fresh straw.

In the tack room squats a rust streaked, left-for-dead Frigidaire. It leans forward, hunched like an old man, and shoulders a boom box. Inside are meds, supplements, and birthing supplies. The old cassette tapes and CDs his granddad played for company on the long March mid-wife nights are stacked on the egg tray in the door. Rubber Soul, Harvest Moon, No Fences, Lost Herd, Some Girls, Sticky Fingers, Born In The USA, Blood On The Tracks.

Wade sets out the surgical iodine, plastic sleeves, Nolvasan disinfectant, and J-Lube before carrying three buckets to the house.

While the pails fill with hot water, he punches in the phone number to the Elks Club. The bartender, Spike, who always sounds like he's talking through one of those voice boxes, says to try the O'Aces. And bingo.

"Yeah," Dwain answers.

"Your cows are calvin'."

"Yeah?"

"Yeah."

"Yeah, well, deal with it and quit bothering me with this crap. I'm busy here hammerin' out a business plan."

"I'm hungry," Dot calls from the living room.

Wade can't find the number for their regular sitter so he calls Marsha Ham.

"It's Friday night. I have plans," Marsha tells him.

"I'll pay you double."

"And?"

"Get them a pizza and one for yourself."

"And something to drink."

"And something to drink."

"And a movie."

"And a movie."

"And only if they come over here."

"You'll have to come get them."

"In this weather?"

"I got a first-time heifer waitin' in the barn."

"That wouldn't be Glory Schoonover would it?"

"L-oh-l."

"Five bucks for gas money and if I have to chain up I'm not coming."

His two hundred dollars for the night is leaving his pocket fast.

Head down and shoulders low, Wade leans into the wind and pushes for the barn. Steam rises out of the buckets and water splashes onto his shirt and pants. He enters the barn, his eyes stinging and watery from the pricks of snow.

Well, they ain't my cows. You only breed them for the calves. Why bother if you don't care if they breach or freeze. My house, my rules, your chores. F-you and your rules. It's not even your house. It's mom's.

He starts the J-Lube in one bucket. Squeezes the last of the hand soap into a second. Dumps disinfectant and the obstetrical chains into the third. Hunts down some twine to tie up the heifer's tail. Pulls the plastic sleeves up beyond his elbows. Scrubs the cow's hindquarters, tail, vulva and anus with the already cold soapy water. He drenches the calf puller with disinfectant. Grabs one gob of J-Lube after another to lubricate the sleeves, the heifer's birth canal, and the calf's front feet and head.

Wade's never used the calf puller on his own. A lot can go wrong. Don't put the chains on right and you can injure, even break, one of the calf's feet. Don't take your time and you can tear up the mom.

His grandfather was always there to talk him through. After Wade's first delivery, his granddad declared it Miller Time and at two in the morning on a school night, they split a Henry's. It was his first, best beer. And the only one he ever had with his granddad.

This could take two hours, but if he's lucky, he'll be done in an hour and on his way to Glory's.

Before putting on the chains, Wade tries to help her dilate. He slides one hand on each side of the calf's head and gently works his hands and arms in and out for a few minutes.

He loops the chains above the calf's fetlocks and the half hitch between its hooves and pasterns.

Work with the cow, his grandfather kept saying. Don't rush.

Each time she strains, Wade cranks and pulls from one leg of the calf then the other to walk the shoulders out.

That's a big freakin' head, a real monster. He cleans the mouth and nose. The bull was too big. If they're all like this, there's going to be some long nights and a stack of stillborns.

He smears on more lubricant. And to avoid tearing any tissues, he stretches the lips of her vulva over the calf's head.

One night Wade watched in helpless horror as his granddad cut a calf out with a saw. There was no beer that night. Just tossed cookies.

He pulls horizontal until the head is out. Goes down on one knee and pulls downward towards her hocks.

The shoulders clear.

Halfway out is a dangerous time. There's always the chance of hip lock.

Wade rotates the calf a quarter turn. That way the wide part of the baby's hips will pass through the wide part of the mom's pelvis.

Steam rolls off the calf and out of the birthing canal like smoke. Wade sweats in the cold. Onto straw the calf slides. The bug-eyed heifer finally collapses.

With two fingers he clears the mucus and fluids from the calf's mouth and nostrils. He then tickles its nose with straw to make sure it's breathing and dips the navel with iodine. By the time he cleans the chains and puts everything away, the cow is up and licking the newborn.

He guides the calf to her nipples.

"There you go, momma."

He checks the calf in the truck before heading into the house. It sits behind the steering wheel like a big black puppy and waits. Waits in the dark and freeze of February for life to show it the way.

• • •

The dirty laundry tumbles onto the kitchen table. Wade uses the plastic bins along with some cardboard boxes that he crushes flat to build a makeshift pen next to the washer and dryer. He removes the garbage, recycling, dog food, bottles of bleach, detergent, household sprays, cleaners, rat poison, boots, shoes, jackets, gloves and hats. Anything the calf might get into.

He spreads newspaper over an old blue tarp from the barn (there will be shit).

"What are we gonna do for dinner?" Dot asks.

"Pizza and a movie."

"Yay!"

"At Marsha's."

"Yuck."

"Do we have to?" Jay Ray whines.

"Sorry. Tough love."

The calf is still in the driver's seat. Looks at him like it knew he would be back. Wade easily flings the mellow, malleable mound of fur over his shoulder and hauls this trusting soul to the mud room.

He towels off the calf and runs his mom's blow dryer over it. It tries to suckle his fingers.

Wade mixes up the colostrum and bottle feeds the newborn. He douses the navel with iodine and heads for the shower.

Wade rips off fifty pushups while he waits for the water to get hot. He normally does one hundred each night. Same for sit-ups, plus twenty-five pull-ups.

The scent and scrub of the fancy French soap is luxurious. Same for the organic lavender-rosemary shampoo and juniper-cypress bath and body oil.

No wonder girls like this junk.

He cracks the bathroom door and wipes the steam from his mirror to shave. Not that he needs to. He has more blackheads than whiskers. But he enjoys this grownup ritual and the tingle on his face from the shaving gel.

The razor easily clears the peach fuzz. The trick is to keep from lobbing off the head of some pimple and starting a gusher.

Wade plays with his hair. Gets it just so. He clasps his hands over his head. Flexes his brick biceps and concrete pecs. Checks out his well proportioned shoulder pad delts. The result of five hayin' seasons of moving miles of irrigation pipe and throwing tons of ninety-pound bales of hay.

Marsha Ham stares through the crack.

Wade puts his thumb and forefinger together and practices kissing.

"You know your French?" Marsha says, pushing her way in. "I could probably help you with that."

Wade grabs at the towel. "Do you mind?"

She takes a seat on the toilet. "Got wood?" Lights up a butt. "No rush, the kids are in the car."

"I'll get your money."

Marsha is three years older. A little flabby but not bad, though she does creep him out a bit. She's in the nursing program at the junior college and is already dressing in that frumpy pajama style that health care providers seem to prefer. She snoops through his shaving bag. "You're a real girly man," she calls after him. "When do I get to babysit you for the night? It's been awhile."

• • •

Wade snaps the tags from the new Levi's, pricey white cotton shirt, black Calvin Klein under shorts and white Banana Republic tee. The smell of new clothes pleases him. Nothing but the best for tonight.

Tucked underneath his bed is an ancient hand-tooled garment bag. Inside is a charcoal black suit with faint gray pinstripes. He pulls it out and rolls his thumb and fingers over the fine fabric. Elegance oozes. His grandfather gave it to him last Fourth of July.

"One hundred percent I-talian wool." His grandfather explained. "Medium lapels, three button, single vent, silk interlining, sharp, clean lines at the shoulder, fitted under the arms, tapered at the waist with a slight flair. A bespoke is what the English call them, custom fitted and hand cut by a little ol' Chinaman from Hong Kong in a tiny back room, back-alley joint in the New York garment district. It'll never go out of style."

"New York? When were you in New York?" Wade cannot imagine his grandfather out of the valley, let alone in a place like New York.

"1953, on my way home from France, where I finished out Korea."

"What was that like? What did you do there?"

"Went to Yankee Stadium, saw Mickey Mantle and Yogi Berra beat the Red Sox, went to Central Park, the top of the Empire State Building, the Statue of Liberty, saw Wonderful Town on Broadway with Rosalind Russell and Edie Adams – "why don't you pick one up and smoke it sometime?'"

Wade doesn't get it. He's too young to be familiar with the tag line for Muriel cigars or Edie Adams, who did the Mae West voice. "I meant in Korea," Wade said, "in the war."

"I know." The old man said, barely a whisper. Wade followed his grandfather's gaze to the hand with the tops of two fingers missing and the quilted web of scars and melted skin that run up under the sleeves of the Wrangler work shirt. "Every evil I know, I learned in the military." There was a long silence, the kind you know not to interrupt. "But Paris…Paris almost made up for it."

Wade slides into the jacket. The sleeves are short and the fit through the shoulders is a little tight, but the quality of the cloth and cut lift him up, changes the way he holds himself, the way he moves, makes him aware of his own presence. Makes him feel good.

Before leaving, he boots up his Mac, clicks on a file. "Phalaenopsis schilleriana," says a mechanical tin man voice.

"Phalaenopsis schilleriana," Wade repeats, "phalaenopsis schilleriana."

• • •

The road out's hard to see. The ruts swallowed by snow. He inches forward, fearful of getting stuck.

Almost as if drawn in by the strands of the high beams, a cow floats into focus. Snow and fog skip around her like smoke. She staggers like a drunk, glares into the grille — a defiant thousand-pound barricade of black.

He lets the bumper kiss her. She lurches aside with a woeful holler. Her sac's broke and a tiny hoof's poking out.

Nope. No way. You're on your own.

He checks the rearview mirror as he passes. Sees nothing but a black hole.

Out at the gate, he looks back. Stares down at the ground, his grandfather's boots. God calls. Guilt. Obedience. Duty.

Aw, alright.

He slams the gate. Yanks the stick into reverse. And with the gearbox wound tight and whining, the steering loose and traction slipping, he retraces his path, flailing backwards into the white confetti.

The truck skids up to the agitated cow. Her head thrashing, tongue lolling and mouth foaming.

Ain't none of this right. Not even the presentation of the calf.

The flashlight reveals a second hoof and a third, which is pointed up. It should be pointed down like the other two. There's no head either. Normal is the head resting on two front legs in a diving like position.

If it's not twins, it's a twisted mess in there and she'll need the vet for a C-section.

Stupid cows. Stupid stepdad.

Back in the barn, Wade sheds the suit coat. Stomps his boots through the leggings of the frozen Carhartt overalls. Punches his arms through the sleeves and gathers up the birthing supplies.

The jars of lubrication, disinfectant, and iodine bounce onto the kitchen table and the buckets clank into the sink. Once again, he uses the phone as the hot water runs. "Hi, it's me."

"I'm sorry."

"What?"

"I don't know who this is."

"Glory?"

"Glory's unavailable at the moment." It must be her mom.

"Could you tell her that Wade called and let her know that I'm runnin' a little late?"

"I wouldn't worry, she's nowhere near being ready. You'll be fine. We can't wait to meet you. Glory has said such interesting things about you."

Before leaving he hunts under the sink and out in the utility room for more soap. The Ivory Liquid dish soap will have to do.

He throws a bale of straw into the bed and plows back out to the cow.

Glory has such interesting things to say about you.

Fortunately, the heifer has not strayed. She meets the headlights head on. She's jumpy, a handful to get haltered and tied.

She's a noisy one, too. What is she telling him? That it hurts? That she doesn't know what's happening? Or maybe she's telling him to butt out. That she can do it herself.

But she can't.

He unzips the coveralls to the waist, pulls back the shoulders and frees his arms. The empty sleeves bob at his side, a useless pair of limbs.

Off comes the new shirt. He folds it with care and places it on the seat next to the suit jacket. The new tee stays put.

The wind whistles, spitting snow and freezer burns.

Wade does the drill: Disinfects the chains and puller. Scrubs her rear. Lubricates the long-sleeved plastic gloves, the calf legs, and her uterus.

He reaches into the birthing canal. About halfway in up to his elbow, he feels a head folded back to its left side. The pressure the cow exerts on his arm is tremendous. He shakes it off. Follows the leg of the hoof that's pointed up. Finds a tail and a fourth leg.

Definitely twins.

And this one's coming out backwards.

Geez, I'll never get out of here. And they'll never get out alive.

They're jammed together, one of top of the other, blocking the birth canal. He'll have to push them further back into the uterus in between contractions. But first he needs to correct the twisted head. He's a virgin at all of this, too. He just warriors up.

He was never in Glory Schoonover's league anyway. After applying more lubricant, he locates the head, cups its muzzle, and turns it into the pelvis with a soft hand so he won't fracture its jaw.

Once the twins are repelled, the heifer folds, collapsing with a bone-rattling cry.

Wade goes down with her.

By now the efficient circulation of young blood combined with an unbending focus on the job at hand mask the arctic conditions and burning cold.

The backwards twin is most at risk. So he takes it first.

More lube goes alongside the calf and as deep into the birthing canal as he can spread it. He blows on the icy chains and rubs the links to warm them before attaching them to the calf's leg in a double loop above the fetlock joint. Inch by inch by steady inch, click by click, Wade coaxes the calf out. The hindquarters take some stretching and turning, and once they clear comes the most critical part. The calf could suffocate because the umbilical chord pinches off before the head is out.

Wade has to work fast. But no so hurried that he tears up the heifer's insides or crushes the calf's ribs against her pelvis.

The cold is quick to steal the baby's steam.

It looks dead. A lot of them do at first. Limp and bluish, glassy eyed. He lifts it up by the back legs to drain any mucus and fluids. He then lays the calf on its side, stretches out the neck and head. Clears the nose and mouth, rubs the chest and lifts the front leg to stimulate breathing.

Nothing. Nada.

He puts his hand behind the left front leg and feels the chest for a heartbeat that isn't there.

The other calf is nosing its way out. He should grease them up, but decides to go mouth to mouth on this one. Just last spring he watched his grandfather bring one back with resuscitation.

So why not?

How they survive the shock of dropping from the warmth of the womb and into sub freezing temperatures in the first place is a miracle.

Wade blows his air deep into the calf's throat and rubs its chest. Forty times he blows. Strong, deep, and concentrated as if nothing else in the world matters. Tells himself a dozen more. Does thirty.

His fire does not spread.

The other calf stands and shivers. Wade picks the birthing sac from its face and unties the wide-eyed heifer. He steps out of the Carhartt's. Uses them to blanket the calf and lays the whole bundle on the seat.

He drags the stillborn out of the road. Brushes away the snow, makes it a bed of straw. Who knows why? For a shred of comfort, even in death?

Back in the mud room it's toweling, blow drying, and bottle feeding at a frantic pace. While dousing the new one's navel with iodine, the cap pops off and the smelly purple liquid explodes all over.

He tries Glory again. But now the landline's out. Probably the storm. Or another unpaid bill. What's the difference?

He swishes a double dose of the Western Family version of Listerine in his mouth and scrubs his hands with the disinfectant soap. The rusty orange iodine stains are stubborn, outlining his fingernails and highlighting his lifelines.

• • •

The heifer is still down. The way the snow circles her big black eye sockets and clings to her ribs and spine, she looks like a puffy Halloween skeleton lying there. If she doesn't stand within a couple of hours, she'll bloat and die.

With the tractor out of commission, there's not much he can do. Still he tries. Wade hooks a shoulder into her rear flank and pushes from the corners of his feet up through his hamstrings, glutes and traps. She claws for earth, digging for traction, snorting and bawling. Her rear end rises but cannot hold, her hind legs Jell-O. Those handmade Luchesses finally lose their edge and ski away from Wade. He bites the earth chin first. Splits his lip. Eats ice and manure. Tastes his own blood. Picks himself up.

The cow lays there. Ragged breathing. Eyes lost.

"I'll see what we can do when I get back."

Something inside him keeps saying this ain't my problem, I shouldn't have to deal with this. This is for the grownups.

He flicks away shit and straw. Spit cleans a patch of afterbirth goo from those new 501 blues. Glad he wasn't wearing the shirt and jacket.

Stupid cows. Stupid stepdad.

Three

The Schoonover place sits at the tip of the lake on the new golf course. You can see the 11th green from their pool and patio.

Wade turns left just beyond the Jesus Is The Reason sign and drives through the open security gate and past the boarded-up guardhouse. All of the cookie cutter spec homes with giant garages that dwarf the entryways and picture windows appear dark and empty.

But not the Schoonover's.

Their well-lit driveway arcs around one of those Japanese gardens where they rake the gravel. In the summer, the shrubs have an Edward Scissorhands-style cut. Now they look like monster white mushrooms.

Their four-car garage is a two-story cottage with a covered walkway leading to a larger, lodge-like main house.

Fresh tire tracks roll out of an empty stall. Inside sit a silver Range Rover and Glory's little white BMW. The tracks must be her mom's cream Escalade.

Hoping to minimize the truck, Wade parks in the shadows alongside a tarped cabin cruiser. He grabs the orchid and leaves the engine running and the heater moaning.

Wouldn't it be cool if her parents said, here are the keys, take one of our cars. Boat out front, Rover in the garage, barbecue and golf course out back. Sweet.

Wade rings the bell. "Phalaenopsis schilleriana," he says as he waits.

"I'm here for Glory." Wade extends his hand, "Wade Summers." The man ignores it, looks back over his own shoulder, then back and beyond Wade.

"Those your wheels?" So much for keeping the eyesore out of sight.

"Ah, well, not exactly. My car, my real car is in the garage." Oh, geez, what did you say that for? Where did that come from? No actually, my car is still on some lot or more like it is being run into ground as we speak.

"I collect myself. Have a 64 Mustang and 69 Mako Shark, three fifty, three fifty. What year?"

"It's a 53. Sundance had one in a catalog for 35 grand.

"Nice jacket."

"Thank you, sir."

"Where'd you get it?"

"Hand tailored in New York, a bespoke."

"Not familiar with that brand." Mr. Schoonover keeps glancing back over his shoulder. "So what is it your father does?"

Good question, sir. I'm glad you asked. No one knows a thing about the unknown sperm donor who knocked up my mom at 15.

"Oh lots of things," Wade says, taking the path of least explanation, "some contracting, runs a few head, fills in at the radiator shop down at the Collision Center. How about you? You're a dentist?"

"Oral surgeon." He says right before a nearby toilet flushes. "So where is it you live?"

"Out Slack Pile Road."

"By the dump?"

"No, no, that's over on Hog Eye."

"A group of us at the clinic have some duplexes out that way."

"Oh I know those, by the sewer ponds."

The cold is starting to penetrate. Guess he's going to make him wait outside. Footsteps approach. High heels clacking on tile. Wade lifts in anticipation. His smile grows. Only it's not Glory. It's Mrs. Schoonover, an older version of Glory adjusting her skirt and puckering her lips to even out her lipstick. She hands her empty wine goblet to her husband. Clamps her arms.

"This is him?" Her eyes burn up and down Wade, the makeup on her face disdain and disapproval. "You showed?" Wade glances at his boots, spots manure and crud, nonchalantly rubs the toe against the back of the heel. He doesn't think they notice. In fact, Mr. Schoonover has disappeared.

"Your hands are filthy."

Damn. "Oh, it's just iodine." He holds up his free hand, turns it in and out.

"Whatever for?"

"Newborn calves, the belly buttons."

"You're late. She's gone, long gone, went ahead without you. And don't think for a minute that you're going to go and make it up to her. I forbid it. Where do you get off? Standing up someone like Glory?"

"I called and…"

"The world does not wait for farm boys. And this weather. He should have drove her, but she wouldn't have it, she was already humiliated enough. I just pray she doesn't get stuck or in a wreck."

"Me, too. I'm sorry," Wade says, backing away, wanting to bolt.

"No shit you're sorry. You should be ashamed."

"Mother," scolds the golf shirt, returning with a fresh glass of red.

"It just makes me want to swear. You have no idea what we went through. Three Fedex overnights for that dress alone. And please, I can't bear the suspense, just what is that thing?"

"It's an orchid."

"Good Lord, he brought a twig." She cocks her head to one side, spins, and sways away, heels clacking.

He feels so small. But not small enough to have disappeared, to have gone invisible.

"Here." Mr. Schoonover says, holding out his hand. Wade automatically takes the white card. "In case you ever want to improve your smile or need a root canal."

The door closes. The lights go off.

Wade flicks the business card into the back of the pickup and turns back toward the entryway. "What about her card, in case I need my ass reamed."

•••

The old Ford mules through a tunnel of snow. The flakes attack the truck like a swarm of cotton balls, dart into the headlight beams, lift up and over the hood and windshield.

Once he crosses the bridge and gets beyond the river, the fog thins. The lights from the high school parking lot burn in the distance. From afar, they glow like a small prairie blaze, flattened and muted by the blowing frosted retardant.

Wade parks next to Clinton Clank's rig. There's a dead horse in the back with a hind leg pointing out at about sixty degrees.

Now, how'd he get that in there?

Over in the teachers' parking lot is the Schoonover cream Escalade.

The black hearse from Orloff's funeral home fishtails into the back of the lot and carves a big swath through the virgin snow on the practice field.

That fool's gonna get stuck.

After a couple of donuts the driver guns it for the gym. The brakes lock and it starts a sideways slide right for Wade.

He calculates which way to dive to dodge the long black coffin. The ass end drifts towards him, then abruptly spins back away and slams into the curb, parallel parking itself in the tow away zone.

Kent Orloff, wearing a tux, aviator sunglasses and a chauffeur's hat, stumbles out. The Black Eyed Peas sing from the speakers.

"You damn near hit me and I'm late enough as it is."

"A deer caught in the headlights dude, but I got your back," Kent says to Wade as he opens the back door. A wine bottle rolls out, leaps to its death, christens the asphalt.

Out step the Marys. Mary Cummins and Mary Will. Younger Coles follows, lip syncing "I Gotta Feeling."

The Marys do everything together. And tonight it looks like they're doing Younger.

"Nice job Kay-Oh," Younger tells Kent as he puts an arm around each date. "Summers, Mosby got a room at the Hitching Post for a post function. You and Schoonover should swing by."

"Ain't he the shit?" Mary Cummins adds.

• • •

Inside the gym, the DJ from Boulder is on a break and it's guys on one side checking mail and texting and girls on the other side, checking mail and texting.

Hundreds of paper mache hearts of various sizes in red, gold, silver and black dance from the trusses. The chatter echoes off the high ceiling.

A few couples sit at the long plastic tables from the cafeteria, sipping punch from plastic cups and eating thimble sized cupcakes.

All the girls are made up and dressed up. Some in shiny, slinky formals, some in brand new unwashed boyfriend jeans with bling on the back pockets, high heels, layered tops (bras or more showing). Others are wrapped in bedspreads for all Wade can tell.

Some of the guys look like waiters or busboys working a banquet. Others are dressed the same as always: the all-Wrangler-all-the-time cowboys, the hip hop hayseeds in butt-crack baggies, unlaced Pumas or Nikes, basketball jerseys or hoodies, their good ball caps on sideways.

"What's that after shave," Clinton Clank sniffs the air, "old heifer?"

"I see you brung your horse."

"I'm takin' it to the dump afterwards. Maybe you could give me a hand? It'd be on your way home."

"I've got a date."

Clint looks around both sides of Wade. "Am I missing something? Or are you?"

Wade keeps going.

"I got the 22. We could shoot some rats," Clint calls after him.

Glory holds herself and her iPad picture perfect in the spotlight at center court. Her cheer team posse — Lisa Schnee, Tami Klug, Debbie Clineball and Patti Clank — stand by her side like maids of honor, clutching their corsages and smart phones over the school's buckin' bronco mascot.

When she sees him her eyes narrow and her smile sours. Anger knots her beauty. She tugs at her dress and stutter steps for the girls' locker room.

Lisa Schnee blocks his way. "She doesn't want to see you."

"Didn't take long for you to go from sexy pants to ass hat," Debbie says.

"I just remembered — unfriend," adds Tami.

"What's that?" Patti Clank sneers, pointing to the orchid. "Your biology project?" The girls trade giggles.

Wade pushes his way to the entry of the girls' locker room. "Glory," he calls inside.

Silence.

"Aw come on, Glory."

The DJ starts up with a megamix of Pussycat Dolls.

"I'm sorry I was late and you had to drive yourself. I can explain."

Still no answer.

"Glory, please, there was an emergency." He looks at the new homemade sign over the doorway. TATOOS, PIERCINGS, AND BALLS ALLOWED. THIS IS THE GIRLS' LOCKER ROOM. This was in response to the sign Coach Phillips put on the door to the boys' locker room: NO EARRINGS ALLOWED. THIS IS NOT THE GIRLS' LOCKER ROOM. The janitors tried to take this one down, but the girls Gorilla glued it.

"Knock, knock, here I come."

"And what do you think you're doing?" Miss Cooper appears before him, hands on hips, head cocked.

Wade retreats. Miss Cooper, Miss Biology 1965, looks like Dorothy from *The Wizard of Oz*, only in a midlife crisis with too much makeup. Even after hours, she wears the ring of keys to lab cabinets strapped to her hip like a prison guard. Can't have those jars of frogs in formaldehyde and them Bunsen burners getting ripped off.

Lisa Schnee marches up, Tami, Patti and Debbie in tow. Lisa hands him her phone. "You smell like a barnyard."

"You would know," he says as he takes her phone. "Glory?"

"I'm not speaking to you, Wade Summers. You stood me up. My whole night is ruined."

"I didn't stand you up. I'm just a little late."

"I had to be here early, I'm the chair. I could have asked a lot of guys, Wade, but I chose you. Do you have any idea how this makes me look, makes me feel?"

Lisa and the others crowd him. "Don't you have your own dates to annoy?" he hisses at them before returning to Glory. "I called and told your mom."

"I sent five texts and called twice."

"My phone quit."

"An hour Wade, almost an hour." It was more like thirty minutes, but Wade doesn't press.

Glory steps out, crinkles her nose. "What's that smell? Cow poop?"

Lisa snickers as she grabs her phone from Wade and wipes it on her dress.

"That's not chew on your lip?"

Wade touches where he bit his lip. "A scab."

"Yew," Debbie says.

"I had to deliver a couple of calves."

"That couldn't wait?"

"No, not really."

"And I could? Excuse me, I've got to get back." Glory turns to Debbie and the others. "Brad's going to be here any minute. We might be getting back together. He sent me the sweetest Valentine."

Wade extends the potted stem to Glory.

"That's not for me, is it?"

Wade nods.

"Oh-em-gee, what is it? A pot of dirt with a stick in it?"

"It's an orchid."

"Hold it up, a sec." Glory clicks a pic.

"Phalaenopsis schillerianna," Wade tells her.

"It looks sickenopsis," Lisa snorts, "deaderianna."

"I can't pin that to this dress. Couldn't you have just gotten a mum?"

"It's not meant to be pinned."

"Then what's it for?" Glory turns to the girls and they start away. "A dead plant, really?"

"It's not dead. It just hasn't blossomed yet."

The girls move toward the flashing lights and music. Debbie Clineball glances back, blows Wade a kiss, runs her tongue across her upper lip, and gives him the finger.

He rests the orchid on a table.

So much for being unique and different.

• • •

Maggie Kerzenmacher dances by herself to Bob Dylan's "Let It Be Me." She slinks up to Wade, does a seductive sway around him, her eyes locked on his. "Your date get stuck in the toilet? Oh, no, wait, she's stuck on Brad Meade."

Wade pretends to ignore her.

Her hip bumps his, her butt brushes his thigh. "You should be with me, asshole."

"You never asked."

Maggie is an abundant girl-woman. Dense shoulders and deep pelvis. She's big, but not fat-big. She could be one of those full figure bra and panty models. Strap a helmet and pads on her, and she'd hold her own on the football team.

Her parents own a sizeable horse operation, mostly paints and appaloosas. Her dad also sells bull semen. And whenever Dutch Kerzenmacher needs the brute muscle of an adolescent back for haying and fixing fence or a gentle, innocent hand to work the horses, Wade hires on.

"Dance with me," she purrs. "I'm asking now."

"Aren't you with Rodney?"

"Our parents are good friends and you know how my mom can be." She turns towards Rodney, who is piling cake onto a paper plate. "I'm going to dance some with Wade."

Rodney nods as he licks the frosting.

What Wade remembers most about Rodney is that he threw up on their field trip to the slaughterhouse in the sixth grade. Rodney was always the guy you stuck in right field and hoped no one would hit the ball to. He says he wants to be a chiropractor. Wade wonders how someone decides on something like that.

Maggie brings Wade into her chest and her lower body into his. He comes alive, but does his best to hide it.

Despite a simmering undercurrent, they have never danced or dated, Mrs. Kerzenmacher's hawkish eye and Scorpio suspicion have suppressed any chance of spontaneous combustion.

"You're calving awfully early."

"You can tell?"

"They making a man lotion now with hints of cowhide and manure? The iodine on your hands."

"I gotta clean up."

Maggie tightens her grip. "I could come over and help." Her warm breath torches his ear and parts south.

"I had to use the jack twice."

"Jacks are real mean."

"One had twins and only one made it. I couldn't get the heifer to stand."

"She'll bloat and die if she don't."

"I know," he says mostly to himself.

Over Maggie's shoulder he steals a peek at Glory. Brad and she are laughing. She catches him looking. He acts like he's looking elsewhere. She acts like she doesn't care.

"The bull must've been a Mack truck," he tells Maggie. "No wonder he got such a good deal on those cows. Who would do that to somebody?"

"Notice anything?" Maggie shows off a big smile. "I took my bands off for the night." She runs her tongue across her teeth. Blows him a subtle kiss. "Better for you-know-what."

Once, in the sixth grade, Maggie pinned Wade to the ground under a swing and kissed him. It was a wet, sloppy smooch. He felt that some unspoken boundary in their friendship had been violated. It was repelling, exhilarating, forbidden and coveted all at the same time. A few days later in a horse stall when he went to reciprocate, a pissed-off Maggie slugged him and swatted him away. Kiss and hurt. That was girls for you. Kiss and hurt. His mom did that, too.

The song winds down.

Patti Clank appears, motions for Wade. "Glory wants to see you."

Maggie tenses. "Stay with me."

"What about Rodney?"

"I'll take care of Rodney."

"Like the way Glory took care of me?"

"You know what? Screw you, Wade Summers, screw you."

Wade has never heard her speak that way. Angry, hurt and hurtful.

Another song starts up. Lady Gaga. Wade drifts toward Glory. Maggie shrinks into the faceless crowd of dancers.

"Aren't you going to fight for me?" Glory asks. Wade glances at Brad. Brad's an okay guy, he thinks — he doesn't really know him, always saw him as a kind of little preppie on the prairie with his v-neck sweaters and tasseled slip-on shoes.

"Brad didn't do anything."

Glory leans closer. He sees the bloom of her breasts. The gold crucifixion cross on the chain at the hollow of her cleavage. Inhales the sensual fuel of her scent. "I'm not wearing any underwear," she blows into his ear, "and I did it only for you."

The collusion and collision of testosterone and estrogen erupt. Distorts the moment. His face smolders. His brain churns with scenarios: take my hand — no grab her hand, go dance, no leave, get out of Dodge, do not pass go, go directly to anywhere but here, Zit's for burger, Runza's for pizza, Mosby's got a room, or just sit in the truck and talk, shit the truck, we'll find a place, Johnson's Corner, the truck stop, just sit and talk, hold hands, make out, listen to music, say something, do something, kiss her, say something, anything, but all systems are no go, paralyzed by the thieves of courage and all his brain will let squirm from his mouth is, "I don't want to beat up Brad."

"It's not about him. I give up."

"Glory."

"No, too late. Stay away, I mean it, and don't text me either."

"I don't get it. You yell at me for trying to be with you and you yell at me for not trying."

"That's right, you don't get it, you don't get any of this," she shouts out as the music stops. The last part bounces around the gym and off the backboards into the crushing silence that seems to hang forever between songs.

• • •

No one is in the boys' locker room. Wade is alone with the resident dented government-gray metal lockers, the wobbly, whittled wooden benches, and the permanent fusion of sugary soap and chlorine bleach that fails to mask the steady stream of urine, salty sweat, dirty socks and tangy sneakers.

A basketball is wedged under the bench. His hands match its dirty orange.

The throb of the dance beyond the door's a whole 'nother solar system.

The Italian wool jacket smells okay, if not comforting. The jeans are a different story.

He runs a standard issue thin white gym towel under the faucet. The water stays right at freezing and the plastic soap dispensers are either busted, empty or clogged.

He claps the boots together, scrubs manure and crusty birthing fluid from each as well as the remaining crud from the cuffs of the virgin Levi's.

He can't believe how much there was, how much he missed in the dark.

Has he gotten so used to all the shit that he doesn't smell it any more?

In the first aid kit next to the coaches' office Wade finds some rubbing alcohol. It dilutes most of the iodine. A trace remains entrenched in his lifelines.

Now what?

Help Clinton with the dead horse?

Get a burger or pie? Tacos? Check out Mosby's?

Why can't you stand up to her? Say and do what you want to do?

Why can't you stand up to anybody?

With one hand he picks up the basketball and shoots it into the trash can.

Swish.

"We could have used you out there last night," says Coach Martinez from the doorway. "We still could. We're only two wins from state." Coach Martinez also teaches Spanish and History. He rarely fails to mention how the settlement of New Mexico and Santa Fe predates Jamestown and the Pilgrims.

"Yeah, well, you know." Wade studies his grandfather's boots, the detailed stitching, manure stains, cracks and creases before looking up. "What did he say that night you came out to the house?"

"Your dad said you had too many chores to do."

Wade winces at "your dad," holds his tongue, stomachs his distaste.

"What did he tell you?" The coach asks.

Wade flashes on the old brown newspaper clipping and picture in the school's trophy case of their only team that ever won state. His grandfather started at guard on that team. And he was only in the eighth grade.

"Oh, I don't know. I couldn't really say." Now Wade wishes he hadn't asked.

"Couldn't or don't want to?"

"Both?" Wade says while looking down at his hands.

"Okay, bueno."

"Where'd that spic ever get the idea you could play basketball?" As soon as it's out, Wade regrets repeating it. "I'm sorry, Coach. I didn't need to say that. I don't know why I did."

"Maybe you did." The coach says. "Sometimes we have to confront our feelings to find out who we really are."

• • •

Wade steps out of the locker room. The music pounds, lights pulsate, and bodies gyrate.

Glory is up on a ladder trying to re-hook a dangling heart. Wade is sure he detects a panty line. Beyond her another torn heart floats to the floor. Lisa and Patti scurry for it.

"Dude." It's Younger with a Mary on each arm. "Want me to have a little backhand-to-head with Meade?"

"I got it."

"That gum smackin' bitch's nothing but a slut for attention." Mary C says.

"All drama, no climax," adds Mary W.

Miss Barnum, Miss Cooper's English department doppelganger, approaches. "What is going on here?"

"We were just discussing how quantum mechanics collide with Einstein's theory of relativity at the edge of black holes," Younger shouts over a Flo Rida mash-up.

"Ain't he the shit?" Mary C adds.

"You clean it up right now, young lady. This is totally inappropriate."

"What?"

"This."

"This?" Younger says.

"Yes, this. What is this?"

"Ever heard of a double date?" into the raucous raunch and synthetic stutters Mary W yells, "YOLO."

Wade withdraws, leaving Younger, the Marys and Miss Barnum to their entanglement. He looks for Maggie but doesn't see her. Just as he reaches the door he hears a muffled "Wade, Wade Summers."

Instant mortification.

The big white poofy teepee floating towards him is Rosie Stuffle. If there were a giant Pillsbury dough girl, it would be her.

"Don't forget this." She hands him the orchid.

"Thanks." Wade catches a whiff of baby powder and fabric softener.

"Would you dance with me? Please? Just one. It doesn't even have to be a whole one."

Death grip to the throat. Her nickname is Tater Sack Thong Rosie.

"Never mind," she says, "I'm sorry. I shoulda never bothered you."

Hearts are starting to drop all over the place. Some torn, some intact. Glory and her clique finally give up on them.

"Okay," he says.

Tears trickle onto her pale pink lady apple cheeks.

"I said okay."

"I know." Now she is sobbing. A bewildered Wade motions toward the dance floor. Trying not to touch her, he touches her.

"I ain't nothing special," Wade tells her, but she's too busy dancing her ass off. A human cone bouncing in the strobes.

Flo Rida raps. Smartphones flash. YOLO.

• • •

Snow swarms the parking lot lights. Wade places the orchid on a trash can lid.

A dark, slender figure trudges toward him. Black tight skirt, black net stockings and barefoot. A blood red boa snakes around her neck. She carries a red stiletto high heel in each hand like they are hammers.

"Fuck me it's cold." Rochelle Moody pulls a long dark cigarette from one of those shoes. "You have any fire?"

She's a spooky one. Miss black magic voodoo skateboard punk. It's rumored that her nipples are black and her midriff soul patch pierced.

"Don't smoke."

No Ray Bans or black low-cut Chuck Taylor All Stars tonight. Gone too is her day-to-day shredded shock treatment look and pasty vampire vibe of purple lips and charcoal eye make up. Her hair's styled and her lips and nails match the wrap and stilettos.

"What's that?"

"An orchid — and it's not dead and it's not sick."

"Okay."

"Phalaenopsis schillerianna."

"Moth orchid?"

"Pink elephant. Would you like it?"

"Didn't cunt Schoonover want it?"

"Glory's not that bad."

"How come she ditched you for Brad Meade?"

Wade frowns.

Rochelle holds up her iPhone. "Wastebook." There's a pic of Glory with Brad.

"It's not all her fault. She's really okay."

"Yeah, lobotomy by botox, I bet those tits are bought too. Yeah, she's going to make some wannabe mid-level-executive-master-of-the-universe dude a real good trophy wife. Get her own McMansion out there on Dry Lake, Lexus SUV hybrid, Nordstrom card, Costco membership, jet ski in July, downhill in January, a little tennis on Tuesdays, a little golf on Thursdays, a nanny, her skinny double pump vanilla latte no whip, couple of brats on Ratlin, drag her droopy boobs and sorry cookie dough baby butt to Curves for some cardio, maybe some yoga without the meditating-touchy-feely-tofu parts."

There's a part of Wade that wouldn't mind being a part of that picture. It sounds a lot whole better than some home on the range in a double wide.

"I can't imagine what you think of me."

"I don't."

That truth lingers in a long, awkward silence. Rochelle eventually asks. "You know Georgia O'Keeffe?"

"Sophomore with kinky hair?"

"No, not Georgette Wong, Georgia O'Keeffe, the artist. She painted orchids, all kinds of flowers." Rochelle signals Wade for the stem. She holds the plant up toward the light and rotates the container.

"I'm surprised you're not with Kerzenmacher. She's always making a puddle over you."

"We're just…" Just what? Wade doesn't finish.

"Summers, will you give me a ride home? I really don't know what I'm doing here. I don't know why I came. I don't belong here."

"You don't want a ride from me — all I got is my grand-dad's crappy old truck. The heater don't work, the seat's all tore up and it's smelly."

"Wow that really got me wet. Fine. Go ahead. Go back in and hang with your Future Farmers of America and

Ag Club homies and watch Meade dry hump Schoonover. Maybe she'll send you on a tampon run to the Kum 'n Go and while you're at it, you can get one for yourself. Jesus, I walked here, I can walk home. Thanks."

Rochelle tip toes away, barefoot into the snow.

Embarrassment and inadequacy choke off any words.

Before she gets too far, Wade jogs up to her, bends forward and offers his back. "Hop on."

"Giddy-up, cowboy."

They bob in and around parked cars, loping past urine, vomit, and beer cans in the snow.

Rochelle fixes on the mound of fur in the back of Clinton's truck. "What's that?"

"A palomino, I believe."

"Is it dead?"

"Why? You want to beat it?"

"Ha, ha, real Comedy Central."

"By the way, I've never been in FFA or Ag Club."

"I'll post a link."

There's an envelope caked in ice under the windshield wiper.

"Someone got a Valentine. A secret admirer? Let's see."

Wade stuffs it in a pocket without opening it.

"You're no fun."

The cab's a meat locker, the seat a cold block of ice, the floorboards, steering, door handles, gauges, and knobs all frosted.

Wade pushes the starter. Grind, churn, squeal. Grind, churn, squeal. The engine's not biting.

"No lighter?"

"Try the glove box. I think there're some stick matches."

Wade tries the starter again. Rochelle flips through the contents. "Udder Balm? That your Valentine for Schoonover? She definitely has the dairy section, artificial or not. Planned to suck them raw, huh? Any condoms?"

Wade flashes back to Faw's when he chickened out.

"Too bad."

Rochelle comes up with a wooden match, pops the head with a red thumbnail. The sulfur hisses as it sparks. She draws the flame into her cigarette. The engine finally fires.

"What smells?"

"What doesn't?"

"You know she's completely waxed. Yeah, that bush's a Brazilian clear cut. Bare lips and store bought tits. Not me. I'm au natural."

"Aren't you pierced? Down there?"

"On my clit? That's for me to know and for you to find out. What's this?" She holds up a manila envelope. "Metcalf Law Office. Family secrets?"

"Leave it alone. It's just my granddad's old stuff."

"Last will and testament."

"Put it back." Wade reaches across her lap and slams the glove box shut. About a quarter of the envelope remains exposed.

"Sorry, Jesus."

There's a tap on the driver's window.

"Wade?"

Glory.

He cranks down the sheet of frost. It sticks about half way.

"You're not mad at me, are you? I can't stand for anyone to be mad at me. Who is that? Is that Rochelle, Rochelle

Moody?" She says the name like it leaves a bad taste in her mouth.

"You don't know what you're missing, Schoonover, he gives great head."

"I do not — I didn't," Wade answers.

"You are unbelievable," Glory tells him. "You dance with Tater Sack Thong Rosie just to embarrass me, and now this lezbo."

"I'm no carpet muncher," Rochelle says.

"I didn't dance with her to embarrass you. Besides, what about you? You and Brad?"

"Brad…" Glory shuffles. "All Brad wants is blowjobs."

"Sista," Rochelle says, leaning across Wade, "all they all want is blowjobs."

Glory steps back, stuffs her hands in her pockets. Snow gathers in her hair. She looks away. Looks distant. Her jacket flaps.

"I just want more…more meaning in my life."

"We all have a horror of the ordinary," Rochelle confides, causing Wade a slight cringe.

"I thought tonight was going to be so awesome," Glory finishes. Wade wants to get out and hold her. Assure her. Make it all better.

Rochelle rests a hand on his inner thigh. "Is that coat Armani?"

"The gown, too," Glory says, briefly flashing the gown with a curtsy and cheesy smile.

"Sweet."

"This is what you drove?"

"I'm sorry, Glory, I really am," Wade says. Rochelle takes her hand away, slides over to the passenger door. "You could have waited for me."

"Yeah." Glory throws back her head and turns, the movement identical to her mom's. She disappears into the night, into the direction of the gym and the muffled big bass backbeats.

Wade cranks the window up. Rochelle rubs her feet with the wrap. The defroster moans.

"She could use some serious ego modification, though she is definitely not fashion disabled. And you, and your 'I'm sorry.' You're a wuss. Shit, my feet are starting to really hurt."

"Give 'em here."

"She wants you to run after her, sweep her off her feet. Go if you want, I could give a fuck."

"I'll warm them up." Wade blows into those baseball mitts of his and rubs them briskly.

"I just wanted to do something different for a change, socialize with my peers. Go to at least one school dance, not skip out on all the marker events of my formative years, have something nice to remember, you know — dress up, have some fun, hang out and rock out. But I just get shut out and made fun of by these a-holes."

"You know what I think? I think you kill, Rochelle."

"Really?"

"This look is much better than the death-warmed-over thing."

"Don't be a butt." She kicks at him and he catches her foot. Takes it into his hands and begins to rub, real slow and tender. He grabs the afghan, wraps her feet in it, and continues the massage.

"Here, wait." Rochelle hikes up her skirt and wriggles out of the black net stocking panty hose. "Before they run." She leans back against the passenger door and places her feet in his lap. Wade's rosy cheeks tingle with flashes of heat when he realizes that she has nothing on underneath.

"Are you blushing?"

"No."

"You're blushing, Wade Summers. I didn't think anybody did that anymore."

"How can I be blushing in this deep freeze? It's too dark for you to tell."

"I can see more than you think," she says. Her toes are stubby but spread out. He notes her hands, tiny like a child's. She's lean but not bony. Good conformation. Hardball breasts and a tight round bottom. Wade presses a thumb into her sole. "You danced with Rosie Stuffle. Wow, cojones grande." The cab is beginning to thaw a bit. "Man, I can't wait for graduation and to get out of this dump."

"What are you gonna do?"

"California here I come. Woo hoo. Already have my ticket. I'm leavin' on a jet plane and never comin' back again. I got accepted to the LA Art Center. It's costing my grandmother a fortune. How about you?"

"I don't know, get a job, hang out, go to school in the fall. I applied with the Forest Service to fight fire."

"You're going to college?"

"You surprised?"

"No, you just don't seem the type."

"I'm probably not. It's just the JC."

"What are you going to major in?"

Wade shrugs and moves to her other foot.

"What'd your counselor say?"

"Herb? Big Herb Anderson, baseball coach, Mr. Shop."

"The flat top on steroids?"

63

"Yeah. We met once. He looks at my file and asks me if I've ever considered a technical school. I don't know what they teach at technical schools. Writing code? Web design? Welding? I don't know and he doesn't say. He also says that given my background, I might want to think about a career in agriculture. Given my background? As what? A teenager growing up on a small cow-and-calf deal? Well, I already know all I need to know about shovelin' shit, stackin' shit, feedin' shit and fixin' broken shit."

Wade works Rochelle's ankles, kneads her calf muscles. "I saw you at that open mic," he says. She freaked everybody out by doing "God Bless America" and "Here Comes The Bride" with big ass Jimi Hendrix fuzz and feedback.

"I know. You were the only one who clapped. That was sweet. I know you were only being polite."

"No, I really liked it, especially when you did the unplugged old Bruce Springsteen."

"Thunder Road."

"Yeah."

"It wasn't too dyke?"

"No, not at all."

"Yeah, that was pretty cool."

She pivots her legs away and comes into him with a mouth full of tongue.

Instantaneous combustion.

A full frontal mash up from lips to hips, her vortex voracious, his every cell ablaze. She presses a breast to his mouth, arches into him, licks his ear, her wet mouth spreading fire. He kisses, squeezes, nibbles and presses back. She guides his hand and rides his finger. She's soakin' wet, a kitchen sponge with a warm slit. How explosive, how intense, how transformed, how consumed, how contagious, how undeniable and electric her charge. Wade is launched into orbit. This must be the way it's supposed to be. Breathtaking and breath-catching. A total red-hot, all out, out of mind, out-of-body into body mind melt.

Rochelle bucks, bends, and with a suck of wind, shudders. Wade churns, damp with the stickiness of life.

The night howls.

• • •

They hold each other's heat. Hang onto the moment by hanging onto each other. Nerve endings cool. The world that spun off of its axis floats back. Time resumes its tick. The engine idles. The heater hums. There's another tap on the window. A loud tap.

"Fuck me." An agitated Rochelle leans over Wade and rolls down the window. "If I throw a stick will you go away?"

"Ma'am?" says a uniformed deputy.

"Sorry, thought you were someone else."

"ID?"

Wade digs for his driver's license. The deputy holds it up to the flashlight. "Aren't you Dwain Creed's boy?"

"My mom's married to him."

"What's in those bags?"

"Old tools and junk."

"What do you use these for?" asks a second deputy, holding up the metal cutter.

"To cut metal?"

"They yours?" the first cop asks.

"They belonged to my granddad. This is his truck and all his stuff. Or used to be. He's dead. He died." Never before has Wade said those last words out loud, and now they hitch in his throat.

"Mind if we look?"

"Nope."

"Those bitches should have a search warrant," Rochelle says as she slithers back into her panty hose.

The deputies poke their lights into the bags then return Wade's license. "Sorry for any inconvenience."

"What are you looking for?" asks Wade.

"There's a lot of illegal consumption, contraband."

"I'm looking for some contraceptives, you have any?" Rochelle asks.

"Good night."

• • •

Fog and snow bury the highway, black ice in the turns. They ride in silence, exchanging glances and shy smiles. Rochelle holds a cigarette out the window. Nonchalantly Wade runs his finger along his nose. Her scent is inflammatory. It's something he recognizes without ever having smelled before. He never wants to forget this night. He never wants to wash his hand or change his underwear.

"Which way? I don't know where I'm going."

"You know where Reliable Plumbing is?"

"By Burns Mortuary?"

"The mansion before that." She puts her hand on his leg and smiles at him. "You don't have to walk me to the door."

"I want to."

"There's no need, really."

"What's it like living by a funeral home?"

"What do you mean?"

Wade just shrugs.

A couple of blocks away, he thinks about pulling over, just to prolong this feeling, this night, being with her.

"The one with the light on."

Maybe he'll park in the dark on the other side of the street, ask her out on a real date.

"Shit, keep going, don't stop," Rochelle shouts and ducks down.

"What?"

"Go!"

Wade guns it. His peripheral vision catches an old Porsche in the driveway. "What is it?"

Rochelle peeks back, not raising her head above the seat. "It's just this guy."

"What guy?"

"Just some guy. You don't know him. He's older."

Wade comes to a dead end. Bare chokecherry and serviceberry branches overwhelm an abandoned car body. Smashed out windows. Hood, wheels, engine block and doors missing. A brown stained mattress up against the trunk.

"I'll go with you."

"I don't think so. He won't take it well."

"I should go with you. You shouldn't be afraid to go into your own house."

"It's complicated. It's over, it really is, he just hasn't moved on yet and I don't want to drag you into it."

"I thought I already was."

"You are. You are," she says softly and runs her hand along his cheek.

"I can take care of myself."

"Let me go, okay? For me." She presses a finger to his lips.

Wade sifts through the trash bags for the rubber boots. Their tops flop against Rochelle's knees as she tramps into the fluttering snow. She grips the red stilettos like hammers just as she did earlier outside the gym. She stops and looks back. "Thanks for the ride, Summers, especially the first one." For all Wade can tell, there was no piercing, but he'll never tell. Then she adds, "It's like anything that's weird—living next to a funeral home, dead bodies – after awhile it becomes normal. It shouldn't, but it does."

Without Rochelle, the cab seems colder.

Wade stalls a few minutes before crawling the Ford down her street. He shuts off the lights, glides to a halt. Scans the house for signs of trouble. Lets the motor idle. Follows someone else's footprints through the yard so he doesn't leave any tracks of his own. Tip-toes up to the picture window. Feels a little peeping Tom creepy and cannot bring himself to snoop. Decides to honor her request and back track. Grinds his way for home.

Four

The downed heifer is still a dark hump in the road.

Tire tracks run up to her back, reverse and go around. There is no blood or broken hide. She's still alive, but her breathing is forced and irregular. Her tongue lolls, glued to the snow. The snowfall has relented some, but not the frigid wind. Wade works the tongue loose. He'll change clothes, then try to get her up.

A murky yellow light leaks from the front room windows. He hopes his mom and Dwain are passed out.

The calves in the mud room eye him as he enters. Expectant, like he's their nursemaid, which of course for now, he is.

The flat, dull light of the overheads punctuates his dread.

Dwain sits shirtless, anchored to the couch, a cigarette clamped in his fist. He nods into the emptiness beyond his nose. Coiled at his knee is the leather belt with the barbed edge buckle and lone dull fang — a copperhead lying in wait. Wade's been bit before. Last time he got three stitches in his left ear, not just from the belt whipping but also a pointed boot toe square to the head.

The lumpy oversized cushion slumped next to him, spread eagle and drawing flies, is his mom. She's naked under the black kimono robe with the loud oriental floral print and screaming tiger.

There's broken glass, pizza crust and French fries under the coffee table. On top are Burger King bags, a greasy pizza box, half-eaten slices, specks of mushroom, chunks of cheeseburger, decapitated Bud Light longnecks, a passed out bottle of Cuervo Gold and a smashed fifth of Black Jack.

The frozen chicken from the kitchen sink is now a dimpled, rubbery blob on top of the TV. The standup ashtray is on its side. A few of its prisoners make their escape.

After a deep drag, the man shoots a series of smoke rings into the woman's face. And just for grins, taps ash into her mouth.

The zombie hacks. And rises.

One of her torpedo tits flops out. Barefoot and bent back, she swats and grips the air for balance, sidesteps the shards of glass, the ashtray, the lamp, and Lazy Boy.

Acid seeps into the son's stomach. He doesn't like it when she's this way.

At the hallway she abruptly turns and glares back at him, "Where's that afghan?"

Wade locks on Dwain, who squints his way.

"Jay Ray and Dot are at Marsha's," Wade says.

"Marsha doesn't know her ass from a hole in the wall. You know Bet caught her humpin' a door knob." She leans into the laminate wall and slides away.

Dwain clicks his tongue.

Wade holds his stare.

"There's calves in my house and a downer in the road."

More acid to rot the gut.

"Your mother nearly piled the Buick into it." He drops the cigarette into the stump of a broken off longneck. "And I thought I told you to shovel the snow off the shop." He starts to finger the belt.

"I'll get to it."

"Damn straight. You'll get to it right now."

"Now?" It's midnight. It's quit snowing.

"Are you deaf? Get your ass out there and right now."

From the back of the house comes a thump-thump-thud, big whimper and groan.

Mother load down.

Dwain bolts up. Holds up his hand like a traffic cop signaling Wade to stay put, then points to the mud room. "And get those calves out of my house. They stink."

Dwain disappears into the unlit hallway.

Wade goes on autopilot and starts picking up after them. He collects the raw chicken and broken empties. Digs pieces of glass out of the sticky carpet. Realizes that he hasn't eaten since school.

"They're your cows," he finally yells. "You bought 'em, made such a big deal out of it, got such a deal on 'em. I don't know what to do with them. You got all that junk takin' up the barn. The bull must've been some franken-steined-Hereford-steroid-Simenal mix. Way too big for those heifers. Granddad never had 'em this early. Nobody does. 'Cause it's the dead of winter. And that downer, you could help me get her up, she's sick and just had twins. She's only worth what? Four, five, six hundred dollars."

Dwain explodes out of the darkness, coming off the lamp like a linebacker shedding a blocker, takes a body blow from the Lazy Boy and as he goes for the leather belt he just keeps on going and pancakes the cheap Target coffee table, its legs snapping like breadsticks.

Wade stands within himself. Adrenaline stoked, awareness acute, fist cocked, heart pumping, muscles twitching.

He wants to rip the man's head off and drop kick it through the picture window and watch it fly to Mexico. That, or mash it into a puddle of sausage and gravy. Maybe go over to the gun cabinet, load a hollow point into the Colt Ghost Commander, place it in front of Dwain and ask him, "You want to do it or you want me to?" And when Dwain says do what, he'll answer with "Put the barrel in your mouth and your brains all over that bookcase."

His mind talks itself quiet. And the weirdest thing happens.

It's like the crash chased off the dark energy and left a space around him, a quiet strength. Durable and undeniable.

Wade softens. Softens and laughs. Laughs at the man at his feet, a sad sack of meat and bones, rank with alcohol, smoke and sweat, staring with bewilderment at the hunk of glass, with the Jack Daniels label still attached, drilled through the palm of his right hand.

There in the density of this stillness, the ticking of the wood stove and the wind rushing outside, Wade feels true.

He glances around. "Granddad?"

"Damn," Dwain fingers the thick shard of glass and shred of label dangling from his palm. He peers into the gouged hand like it holds the secrets of the universe, his face a pearly ash. "Goddamn, look it what you made me do." He burps and gurgles, holding down what he can, while the rest runs in strings out of his nose and mouth. "Ain't you gonna do somethin'?"

"Yeah, I'm gonna go shovel off that shop roof, right now, like you said."

"No."

"You want me to drive you to emergency?"

"No. No fuckin' way."

Wade returns from the utility room with a rusty pair of pliers, a roll of silver duct tape, cotton pads, a box of gauze, and a brown bottle of hydrogen peroxide.

He squats down like a catcher. Takes the gutted hand into his own as if he's about to say grace. Notes the lack of blood. Looks Dwain in the eye and squeezes. Hard.

"So here's the deal."

Dwain yelps and gasps for air. Tries to pull and twist from the boy's grip but cannot. His feet slide back and forth but gain no traction. His eyes talk of terror.

"Easy, big fella," Wade whispers like he's gentling a horse, "easy."

Dwain stays clenched and stiffens into the pain.

"You, now you fry in your own grease, disappear up your asshole but Mom, Dot and Jay Ray, you be real nice to, take care of, and this, all of this here ends, right now, cease and desist, no more 'boy I must have been real drunk.' Comprehende no mi padre? Comprehende?"

Dwain bobs and nods, his voice swallowed by anguish. Wade studies the hand like a palm reader. The thick glass's rammed all the way through and sticks out a good inch just below the knuckles.

Wade yanks it out in one clean jerk.

The wind howls. The house shakes and shivers. The blood runs. Dwain visits the night.

Wade cleans and wraps the wound. "You're going to need stitches," he tells the unconscious.

• • •

His mom's on the floor in his parents' bathroom. Lips to linoleum. Bare ass full moon.

Instant gag reflex.

He pulls down the kimono robe to cover as much of the splotchy butt as he can.

A big blue hairbrush with black spikes sticks out of her head. Clutched in her left palm are a turquoise necklace and hoop earrings. He sets them on the vanity. Notices a wet nest of hair in the sink. From her cedar hope chest, he comes up with a flannel bed coat and wrestles her into it.

"Leave me alone." She slaps at his hands. "No more, not tonight, that well's done dried up, dry as a desert."

"It's me, mom, let me help you."

"Sweet sixteen and never been kissed," she slurs. He loops his arms under her armpits and drags her to the bed, her head at his heart. She turns stubborn, flails like a cranky child, the bed coat and kimono going every which way. Wade stumbles. Goes down with her aboard, tits first to his face.

The boy scrambles from beneath her with an interior primal scream. He's revolted by her nakedness, nauseated by the nipples that once nurtured him.

He shakes it off. Keeps his distance. Gets one of his granddad's old beacon blankets and covers her up. He puts her drug store glasses next to the clock radio with the white oversized numbers and a copy of *The Corrections* with the Oprah sticker on it. The cover smells of hand lotion. Not tonight though. Dry as a desert.

Dwain's still a pile of dirty laundry, a little more throw-up on his chin, some of it green — lettuce, maybe pickle.

Wade empties the gun case — the Colt, the 12-gauge, 30-30, his little brother's 4-10 and 22. Then into a plastic Safeway bag he dumps the ammo. The casings clink and shuffle among themselves, a sack of deadly stones.

Outside, the storm's on a break, the clouds clearing; the temperature gauge points to 21. Wade smiles at the shop roof. No cave-in tonight. No gunshots to the head.

Maybe he can give the tractor a jump and use the bucket to nudge the heifer up.

There's a new stack of doors, a vanity, beige sink, even a new stove and frig, still in the boxes, behind the barn door. What's all this stuff for? Dwain ain't buildin' nothin' for no one.

Wade stores the guns and ammo in an empty feed box.

He doesn't bother with the cables. They won't reach.

He folds the jacket and white shirt over a saddle in the tack room. Pulls up the offending Carhartt's. Puts on his mucking boots and decides against the gloves. The liners smell of horses, and he doesn't want to lose Rochelle Moody's scent. Not just yet.

The frostbitten Ford creaks out to the cow.

If he can make a harness or some sort of sling, work the tow rope around her shoulders and hip, then pull the pickup forward, maybe she'll find the strength to stand. It probably won't work. But you have to try. You always have to try.

The lights spot a coyote at her anus. It tears off into blackness. He's too late. She's frozen dead meat. Just won't make it to the supermarket on a Styrofoam tray wrapped in cellophane.

Damn.

His solar plexus twists.

Damn.

He smacks her ribs with his fist.

Damn.

His eyes blur.

If only someone around here would actually just try. He kicks the big black slab in the belly. Stubs his toe. Retaliates with a kick from his other foot. Stubs it too.

Dammit.

If only his granddad were still alive.

Tears freeze dry.

If only.

He plops down next to the heifer, snow and gravel inches from his eyes. A clump of ice melts down his neck.

Dead quiet. Dead calm. Dead cow.

The wind has pretty much blown itself away. Written on the yellow ear tag is 0107. The first born of 07.

He strokes the crusty fur. Picks at the ice crystals like they're scabs. Feels at fault. Guilty as charged. Maybe he ruptured her insides. Maybe he was too hard, too much of in a hurry. But she looked sick from the get-go. The foamy mouth. The bawling.

He tells her that he's sorry and asks forgiveness.

More sorry than messing up with Glory? Probably not. Why are these always the choices? Yet being late led to

Rochelle. It's like that Apple guy said in that speech: you can only connect the dots by looking backwards.

He wonders how their nights turned out. Glory's and Rochelle's, even Maggie's. Younger's must have been epic.

The stars sparkle though the waning fog.

He tracks the dusty sweep of the Milky Way. Locates the North Star.

The night sky absorbs him.

One of his science teachers, Mr. Looney, said that the stars we can see account for less than five percent of what's out there. The rest is dark matter, dark energy. Empty space that is not empty.

Completely incomprehensible.

Still, all those stars. Billions of nuclear furnaces spewing carbon, oxygen and nitrogen, the raw materials of life into the universe. And all that light? Is it racing toward us or away from us or both?

The past. That's what he's looking at. Light from a source that may no longer be there. Burnt out suns. And the darkness? Is it still there, or is it something else now? And is it headed our way?

Hard to connect those dots.

He remembers three black and white pictures from some art book. One of the Milky Way, one a macro close up of human skin, and one of a Jackson Pollock painting. They looked almost identical.

Maybe it's not so hard to connect the dots after all. Maybe you don't need to connect them.

"May your next life be better," he tells the cow before hauling her stillborn to the burn pile out behind the barn.

For some reason the horse trailer's parked back there with two big old white propane tanks hanging out of the ass end.

• • •

All the doors to the house are locked.

The calves in the mud room doze.

It won't be the first time he's slept in the barn. He considers hiking across the field of snow to his grandfather's house, but it's probably no warmer than the barn. Besides, it's pretty cleaned out from the yard sale. Spoons and forks a quarter each. China a buck a plate, books fifty cents each, hard and paper. Wade grabbed a few of the Classics before they were dumped on the card table out on the porch. He was hoping for the white '65 El Camino but some guy handed Dwain a take-it-or-leave-it money order for quite a bit less than the asking. Dwain took it without much sniveling until it turned out to be a fraud. They never found the guy or the car. His mom nabbed three crisp one hundred dollar bills for the big pine dining table and chairs. They sat in the window at Yesteryear's Antiques for a few weeks before selling for a grand. She got her hair done and a pedicure.

The orchid pops into his mind.

As he retrieves the delicate plant from the cab, the manila envelope sticking out of the glove box catches his eye. Under the lame dome lamp, he reads the will. One section he reads twice. Then reads it again.

In the open stall behind the tractor, Wade makes his bed. Scratchy straw mattress. Burlap feed bag pillows. Stack of saddle blankets. He stays in his jeans and t-shirt but sheds the boots and socks.

Through a hole in the corner of the roof, he can see the stars again. The smell of the horse blankets comforts him. The smell of Rochelle Moody, however faint and fading, comforts him more.

If she only knew where his hands and mouth had been just hours before.

A whirl of images from earlier in the evening catalogs itself into his memory bank, spurring a nonlinear state of dreams and vivid sleep.

He dreams of calves with purple tongues. They're drowning. Drowning in air. How can that be? Then there's Glory playing Glory's mom and vice versa. "I'm not wearing any underwear," Glory's mom laughs at him. Next he's in the thick of it with Rochelle, "Keep going, don't stop." He can feel himself smile until he realizes that it's really later in the truck, that she's yelling for him not to stop at her house. Then he's in an empty classroom. He keeps erasing stuff on the blackboard, algorithms he thinks, but they keep coming back. But not his granddad. Wade keeps riding up to the mountain meadow where they were that day. Every detail huntin' knife sharp. The horse sucking wind. The jolt of the pounding hooves. But his grandfather isn't there. Wade can't find him; he's lost. This is where he's supposed to wake up and go, "It's only a dream." But that day. That day was not a dream. And Wade never really seems to wake from it.

• • •

It was the last day of summer.

They were bringing the cattle down. More like following actually. The older ones like Lottie, one of his grandfather's pets, knew the routine. That or just craved greener pastures and the convenience of regular feeding.

They stopped for a late lunch in a faded wildflower meadow on a plateau called Thunder Rolling. It was like being up on the roof of the world. They fed the horses Fuji apples and garden grown Danvers carrots. Fed themselves homemade granola, Greek yogurt, organic blueberries and bananas with Starbucks French roast and half-and-half for dessert.

"This is about as close to heaven as I'm ever going to get," his grandfather said.

The valley rolled out below. A bumpy suede patchwork of frayed farms, sun dried fields and unfinished subdivisions stitched together by dusty roads, power lines and shiny strips of irrigation pipe.

Lonesome fir, pine and quaking aspens made their stand at the fringe.

The genesis of Sled Runner, the creek that runs the edge of their place, is just a mud seep up here. A watering hole for chickadees, juncos, pine grosbeaks, mosquitoes and dragonflies.

They let the earth warm their backs and the afternoon sun warm their faces.

Wade can still bring up the stillness and silent power of those moments.

Two hawks floated the thermals. The clouds shape-shifted.

"Theoretic physics and finance," his grandfather stated.

Wade waited for clarification.

"That's what I'd look into if I was going to college. They can write an equation, an algorithm for just about anything. Anything but this."

"I'm not so sure about college."

"Of course they won't do you any good without the arts and humanities."

A great western owl flew over. Close enough to hear the swoosh of the slow, steady flap of four-foot wings.

"Can you fly an airplane?" his grandfather asked.

"No."

"How do you know? Have you ever tried?"

Like a branding iron to the cerebral cortex, point made. Overhead, the hawks talked.

"Let yourself go, Wade, let yourself go. Stay around here and you'll keep bumping into the ceiling."

While Wade packed, his grandfather cruised the meadow, uprooting Russian knapweed, purple loosestrife and Canada thistle to burn.

"How you take care of the land is how you take care of yourself," he told Wade as the heads and stalks of the noxious weeds melted to smoke and ash.

"You take 'em on down. I'm going to weed some more, have one last cup."

"I can stay."

"I'll catch you."

Wade thought it odd that they weren't going down together, but didn't question it.

The old man stirred the small fire and whistled for Puzzleface, the lightning streaked black and white Overo paint, ropin' pony and travelin' companion.

Wade slung his saddle onto Kiowa, his mellow appaloosa gelding, and cinched it up.

"Don't forget to drain the tanks, wrap the pipes, worm and shoe."

Huh? What? Everything okay?

"Just thinkin' out loud. Thinkin' ahead."

Guess so, Wade thought, we don't do that for another month. "Isn't there an algorithm for that?" Wade asked.

His grandfather smiled and waved him on.

"I could always go to YouTube U like you," said Wade.

"Get, before the cows beat you down."

Queenie, the arthritic, one-eyed heeler mix nipped about, pushing any laggards into line behind Lottie, the old grand dame who led the cows home.

Torn between the task of her blood and the master of her heart, Queenie scampered back and forth between the herd and the old man. She barked at him, scolded him to saddle up, and he pointed her back to the cows. Finally, her breed and lust for work seized control and she stayed on the small black army, kept it tight, allowing no stragglers.

Wade looked back up at the old man and the horse on the horizon. The sun seemed to be going down on them. He was scratching Puzzleface's ears and rubbing his nose. Their black shapes cut into the orange ball until it flashed and flared and their silhouettes disappeared into the fiery monster and melted into the high mountain ground.

A chill rode up Wade's spine. He was tempted to gallop back up. But something held him back, pushed him to continue on.

The next morning Puzzleface showed up at his grandfather's barn. No saddle, no halter.

"You left him up there all by himself?" his mom said as she boxed his ears. "How stupid are you?"

Geez, he still roped every Sunday. Worked out at the gym. Ate well. He was healthy.

Wade grew more alarmed as he rode. It seemed that the faster he went, the longer it took, and the closer he got, the farther he had to go.

The old man was still on the mountain.

Queenie had come back for him. She was curled at his feet. Mournful and confused. She softly wagged her tail. Wade petted her.

He was in the wildflowers among the bees and butterflies. A ladybug resting on his lip.

His skin was a glossy porcelain.

"Granddad," Wade whispered, as if not to disturb him. He took the bloated body in his arms and hugged. Squeezed hard and cried harder. He kissed his forehead, startled by how cold it was.

Sheriff Moen arrived about an hour behind him. He phoned his office and told them to bring a stretcher, and they hauled him down Indian-style. Wade kept his hat. The hatband's salty sweat never failed to bring up bittersweet recollections.

"Sign the guest book," his mom said to him before the ceremony.

"No. What for? I'm not a guest. I'm family."

"Sign the friggin' book," she hissed through clenched teeth. Wade picked up the pen and faked it. Never put ink to paper.

• • •

The heifer in the next stall blows, jarring him conscious. No longer in his dreams, no longer in his memories. His back to frozen ground. His heart to the sky.

The heifer bangs around. Butts the walls. Shuffles straw. Snorts and shits.

He tosses her a flake of hay.

The calf with the purple tongue is dead, crushed by the weight of its mother.

Wade sags at the discovery. Curses the vacant-eyed cow. Busts up the ice in the water with his fist. The cold drowns the pain. He watches the blood from his knuckles disperse. Sucks on the wound as he refills the tank.

He carries the calf out to the burn pile.

Still visible, The Big Dipper's directly overhead, tilting towards sunrise, pouring out its guts. A parallel universe of farm lights dot the brittle blue terrain. Fog sleeps on the creek. The willows and cottonwoods stand gaunt and ghostly. Black mountains cut into a graying sky. Night fades to day. Wade can see his breath.

He makes a place for the calf next to the other one.

He thinks of them as angels.

They have such a power about them. Such stillness, such silence, such complete and uncorrupted innocence. The perfectly formed hooves, tiny ears, little noses. Their watery black eyes wide open, all-knowing. The stare of eternity. Their miracle interrupted.

There has to be more to life than ground round. Any life.

Under a soft scarlet sky, Wade feeds the herd. Counts two with baggy udders to move to the corrals later. Finds no new black dots in the snow. Smells a skunk somewhere near.

Smoke rises from the woodstove chimney.

Wade grabs the jacket, shirt and orchid. The card that was under the windshield dangles from the coat pocket.

"Kiss me and you'll know how important I am." Sylvia Plath. The handwriting looks familiar.

Wade raps on the back door.

"Lock yourself out?" his mom says without looking at him and shuffles back to the kitchen. "You had to use the good towels? I want this all back the way it was."

He mixes up the last of the colostrum and bottle feeds the anxious inmates. Luckily there's no diarrhea to clean up. He'll need to find a mother to nurse these two. His granddad would take the hide from a dead one and rub it on an orphan. The idea is to trick the momma into recognizing the scent of her own calf on another. Maybe he'll skin the one with the purple tongue. Though that heifer isn't such a good mom so far.

His mom is at the stove breakin' eggs and burnin' bacon. Dwain is at the kitchen table, eating up Craigslist. "Did you do that to him?" she asks Wade.

Wade pours a cup of coffee, adds some cream to cut the bitterness but it's spoiled and curdles.

"You're not talkin' either? He won't go to the clinic. And that carpet and couch? Once blood dries you can't get it out." She flips the bacon. It splatters and sizzles. "That coffee table just up and break itself?"

"I found his will."

His mom keeps her back to him. Slowly turns an egg. "What will?" She serves Dwain, who keeps his head down, immersing himself in the intricacies of removing the fat from the bacon.

"It's not like I'm going to boot you off."

"You pay the property taxes then," Dwain says with a mouthful of egg.

The skillet starts to smoke.

"He bought this house for me," his mom declares. "This is my house, that's his shop and those cattle are ours." She waves the spatula to underscore each point.

Wade foregoes asking for the snow machine and ATV keys. Once the tractor has a new battery, he'll just drag them out.

After a shower and change of clothes, Wade slides his laptop, a few clothes, and his grandfather's boots into his backpack.

"Let me fix you breakfast, hon," his mom says on his way out. Dwain and his plate are gone. "How was your date?"

"I don't know. Okay. I gotta get — we're out of milk replacement."

"Just put it on the account. The phones are workin' again. You want to take the Buick?" She starts for her purse.

"Mom."

She looks back, easily reads him. "Don't."

"What?"

"You know what." She scolds with the spatula. "You don't know what it's like. You don't know how hard it is. You're just a boy. A stupid schoolboy. How would you know? He has some good ideas, he does, it's just that…" her voice falls off. "Besides, who's going to want someone with two kids and this bankrupt crap of a place?"

They let the silence and the unsaid take over.

He doesn't correct her on the number of children or the solvency of the farm.

She trails him into the mud room.

The calves lay side by side up against the washer, front feet folded under their chests, heads erect and alert to every move, every sound. A pair of puppies lost.

She gazes out the window while he pulls on his rawhide boots. "Earlier when you were out there feeding," she says softly, "I thought it was him and then I realized how much like him you are. And I am comforted by that. I truly am."

Wade watches the calves watch him. Slings the backpack over his shoulder and stands up. "So when were you going to tell me, mom?"

"As soon as we thought you were ready. More mature, you know, better equipped to handle it."

"After it was all sold off?" Wade opens the door and walks away. One of the calves pees.

"I told you I had some important papers for you to sign," she yells. "You'd'a gotten your share. I've always taken care of you. Always. And get these goddamn calves out of here." She looks down on the calves. "Ungrateful little shit."

• • •

The FOR SALE sign in front of his grandfather's place is rooted into the frozen soil like rebar into cement.

Wade karate kicks. Jerks it back and forth. The land does not lose its grip easily. The metal sign barely bends.

The real estate agent's shit-eating grin looks more and more like a terrified frown as Wade hooks the tow rope to the sign and pulls it out with the truck.

As he pitches the sign into the irrigation ditch he loses his footing and slides into the snow bank tailbone first.

God, ain't nothing easy.

• • •

Down by the crossroads, Wade passes Sheriff Moen. He's sitting in his black pickup next to a marked prowler pointed in the other direction. Remembering his kindness that morning on the mountain, Wade waves. The sheriff looks away.

Guess he doesn't remember. Or has more important things on his mind.

Wade's first stop in town is Mountain Tire and Tractor Supply. It's in the old Twin Plex Cinema in the no-longer-there shopping mall. In red letters on the movie marquee it says Tire Blow Out Sale. Es hable espanol.

They put a lift in each of the theater bunkers. Kept one row of seats with cup holders and put it out in the lobby across from the wheel display. The old candy counter is now the service desk. They kept the popcorn machine and offer free bags of stale while you wait, along with burnt coffee and powder creamers to float on top of the bitter brew.

While Wade waits for Shorty Gibson to bring out a new battery, Amy Root, who's one year behind Wade in school, approaches and in a low voice asks, "Did you really go home with Rosie Stuffle?"

"No. Just made out in the parking lot."

Amy looks like she's about to throw up.

• • •

Next stop, Barlow Feed and Fuel.

Just follow the pigeons or flies and take a right at the 4" PANSIES HERE FOR SPRING sign.

Barlow's is housed in the tallest buildings in town, the old grain elevator and stoic silos that stand like old silver capitol domes along the abandoned railroad spur.

He pulls up in front of the big plastic greenhouse they erected after they expanded into the old shipping corrals. (Plenty of fertilizer in there.) They left one of the decrepit wooden loading chutes as some kind of monument.

These days Barlow's is more of a pet store and nursery. They cater to the same hobby farmers and gold tinted, silver-spurred horse women on those ranchettes over near the Front Range that his grandfather used to sell his organic alfalfa-timothy mix to.

They still stock a few ranch supplies but mostly carry lawn mowers, peat moss, Miracle-Gro, rakes, shovels and garden hoses. Even display a few of those replica Radio Flyer red wagons. No one Wade knows ever had one as a kid.

Along the back wall are a dozen milky black and white photos framed in gray cedar, probably from the stockyard fencing. There are pictures of trucks loaded with sugar beets lined up at the scales. Train cars piled high with spuds and others being shot full of grain. There's even an old yellow newspaper clipping about sugar beet yields of 290 tons per acre.

Wade has no memory of any sugar beets grown around here.

In the back office, Chad Tally sneaks a bite of a Snickers bar and puts it back in the desk drawer before waddling out to the counter. Part of the chewy nugget sticks to his stringy blonde walrus moustache. He tugs down on the Mountain Dew t-shirt that doesn't quite make it over the belly jelly that hangs over the big silver rodeo buckle.

You'd never know that less than a decade ago, Chad was a champion roper.

"I need a dozen packets of colostrum replacer." Wade says.

"Can't sell it to you. Not an if you don't settle up your mom and dad's account."

"I'll give cash."

"No can do. It's six months in arrears."

"It's not my debt."

"You're name's on the account."

"Is Chet around? Mr. Barlow?"

"He got no say in it no more." Chad married into the business and is slowly taking over.

Wade weighs driving over to Ranch and Livestock Supplies. It's about a 30 minute drive. 45 in the Ford. "How much is it?"

"Hundred an eight even."

Wade does the math and reaches for his wallet. "Just a half dozen, then."

Chad rings up the sale. Marks the account paid in the computer. Gets the pouches.

"You're calvin' early out there."

"What? We buds now?" Wade asks before mentioning on this way to the door, "You got some Snickers there in your 'stache."

Before leaving the old part of town, Wade drives to the library across from the park.

The only person Wade sees on the way is an elderly woman smoking a cigarette outside of the Hair It Is Beauty Boutique. She's wearing a blue cape and has one of those tin foil jobs on her head.

It's a Carnegie Library, a tidy unadorned square red brick building built in 1918. Twelve clunky computers occupy about a quarter of the main room. The high ceilings, polished pine planks and old book smell still lend the place a sacred air of letters.

It doesn't take Wade long to find what he's looking for. Georgia O'Keeffe. Two F's.

He browses her bones, landscapes and flowers.

Since there's only the one book, Wade gets on Google. Reads a few quotes.

"Someone else's vision will never be as good as your own vision of your self. Live and die with it 'cause in the end it's all you have. Lose it and you lose yourself and everything else. I should have listened to myself."

Her abstractions of shells and enlarged blossoms strike Wade as ornate wombs, and some of the landscapes as naked bodies on their sides, the legs pulled up, shoulders smooth, rolling gullies of belly flab.

Maybe that's too much of a hangover from last night. Rochelle and the spreading of pollen. Eyes of the beholder stuff.

"In every painting there is all of your life coming back at you. Not just one flower or piece of bone or sky. That's just what you see at the end when the work is finished but at the start when you see the empty canvas, you see your whole life."

He puts the slightly warped book with the antique pages back on the shelf. Runs his finger along the spine, cracked from the wear of time and use. Goes back to the web. "I have picked flowers where I found them."

Wade asks the librarian for a piece of paper. She says she can't give him any. He wonders why but not enough to ask.

Around the corner from her desk, he scans the bulletin board. Domestic Violence Support Group meeting on

Thursday nights in the basement. A notice about Rural Employment Opportunities (only one phone number tag missing). Someone with vinyl records for sale — EARL SCRUGGS TO JZ. An alert from the Sheriff's department about cattle rustling and property theft (evidently some haystacks have gone missing). Wade makes sure no one is watching and swipes the flyer about some Hoedown at the Herb Farm.

One of the quotes he writes down: "Nobody sees a flower—really it is so small it takes time—we have time—and it takes time, like to have a friend takes time."

It reminds Wade of the orchid.

He looks up Sylvia Plath. Reads a bio and skims *The Bell Jar*.

He likes Georgia O'Keeffe's skulls and pelvises the best. And one called "Ladder To The Moon".

Since it's nearby, Wade decides to cruise by Rochelle's. Maybe he'll run into her.

From a few blocks away, the black Porsche looks like it's still parked in the same spot. Wade notices an ambulance in the alley behind the neighboring funeral home. Two attendants off-load a gurney with a covered body and wheel it inside. He slows down to watch.

When his attention wanders back to Rochelle's, the Porsche is spinning out of the driveway and shooting right for him with Rochelle riding shotgun.

Crap. Now what?

There's no room to turn around. And he just can't back up.

The Porsche lunges by. Rochelle never looks his way. But he can tell that under the Ray Bans she's all daggers.

Bulls kick in his stomach. His face stings from a low grade burn.

He could always say he was coming by to pick up the galoshes. Though he knows no one will ever ask.

Once the Porsche is out of sight he makes a u-turn.

• • •

He stops at Bob Faw Pharmacy for a Valentine's Day card. They're mostly phoo-phoo grandma stuff or dumb jokes.

He counts up the last of his cash. Selects a piece of construction paper. Picks out a glue stick, black sharpie, a packet of red hearts, one of gold stars, a *National Geographic, Vanity Fair, Wired,* and *Red Herring.* Throws in a box of Trojans.

"I can't sell those to you," Mrs. Faw says, moving the rubbers to the side. Mrs. Faw is a tight, severe woman, her gray hair almost a crew cut. She used to teach part time P.E. and Health Sciences.

"How about a pack of smokes?"

"What kind?" she says as she turns to reach behind her.

"You'll sell me a cancerous carcinogenic but not a preventative measure against disease or abortion?"

Mrs. Faw makes sure no one is within earshot and motions Wade to come closer. "Hon," she says in a low voice, "with a big pony like Rose Stuffle, just use a fold of blubber instead of her vagina. She won't mind and you won't know the difference."

"I'm not doin' anything with Rosie Stuffle."

"Well we know you aren't doin' anything with Glory Schoonover, so you really don't have a use for 'em. It's all on the dance page."

Great. Social media octopus distorts reality. Chokes small town boy.

The Ford glides down Frontage Road behind a snowplow. He passes the Spine Institute and Young Forever Surgery Center where Glory's dad has his office. His sign is a smiling mouth with Schoonover spelled out on the teeth.

Wade double clutches and down shifts onto the less traveled White Horse Road. He steadies the truck in the icy ruts until he rolls to a stop in front of the Better Bulls Better Priced sign at the entrance to the Kerzenmacher place.

He rips apart pieces of the magazines and constructs a Valentine card. It looks like a ransom note with red hearts, gold stars and glossy pictures.

The drive up to the main house is lined with old farm equipment. Buckboards, wagon wheels, plows, rakes, cutter bars, ancient tractors, combines and old stake bed trucks. A museum of rust and wood rot.

Mrs. Kerzenmacher answers the door. "Dutch isn't here. Did he call? I don't know of any work."

"Is Maggie home?"

"She's at practice."

"Sorry to bother you."

"You don't need to come sniffin' around here, Wade."

Out on the road, Wade slides the envelope into their outsized metallic mailbox. It's shot full of bullet holes.

Five

Back home, Wade finds the gate wide open. These people, Jesus. He gets out to close it.

The dead cow's still in the road. Ravens laugh on the power lines.

There are several vehicles parked around the mobile. Marked and unmarked.

Dwain's running from the back. Slip slidin' away on the snow. His bandaged paw held high. A deputy hot on his ass wraps him up with a textbook tackle and cuffs him.

What's going on?

His mom is out front with Sheriff Moen. She flicks her cigarette into his face. Kicks his leg and flails at his chest like a human windmill.

This can't be happening.

Yet it is.

Wade's heart runs heavy, his mind spins. His first adrenaline-fueled instinct is to run to her defense, to protect her, to save her.

The sheriff pins her to the hood of a black prowler while one of the deputies from last night cuffs her wrists.

Wade jumps back in the truck. Fires it up. Looks ahead, the scene before him alien and out-of-sync.

Two guys in blue jackets with SHERRIF'S DEPT in big yellow letters on the back come and go from the barn. They are moving all of that construction stuff while another guy tags it and takes pictures with his cell phone. The horse trailer with the propane tanks is now parked out front.

Jay Ray and Dot watch from the mud room. A woman from social services stands behind them, a hand on their shoulders. Wade's outrage and swollen chest of offspring heroics fizzle. An emptiness slowly but inexorably rises within.

A couple of passing cars have stopped to gape.

Dwain's on and off of his knees, feet sputtering as the deputy drags him by the neck of his shirt.

A kind of sadness for the man dulls the boy.

Sheriff Moen gently guides his now meek mom into the caged backseat.

Maybe they'll let him look after Jay Ray and Dot. Probably not. Not legally anyway. He's still a minor and only a half brother. Besides, they'll probably make bail and be back by sun down.

It'll all be in the police blotter for everybody to see.

He shifts gears.

Backs out.

Closes the gate.

Quietly wraps and hooks the chain without looking back.

• • •

The short trip to his grandfather's house seems to take a lifetime. Catharsis at a crawl. Limping out of limbo. Traveling by the speed of a secondhand. Pulse by primeval pulse, breath by purifying breath, the chant of life banging at the inner ear. Red water pumping nourishment, purging neglect. The eyes no longer flinching inward.

He digs the FOR SALE sign out of the ditch. Leans it up against the buck and rail.

He carries the orchid, his backpack and sleeping bag inside.

The farmhouse smells of furnace oil and stale apples. There is ice in the toilet.

His phone buzzes. The Sheriff's department? EZ Pawn and Bail Bonds? No. Just a signal that the phone is working again.

He has a missed call from Younger along with a pretty sexy pic of him and the Marys. Plus eight texts from Glory. The last two from earlier this morning.

whr r u?

ur late!!

HURRY UP!!!

Going w/o u

PS Dn't bother

Pleez dn't b mad G

I miss u

Call me okay? Sad face G

While the potency of her scent, the brush of her gold drenched hair, the shape of those luscious breasts, hide-and-seek nipples, inviting thighs, and tempting ass stoke eternal sparks, he deletes all. Shuts off the phone.

He looks out across the field from where he came. Doesn't see a blank canvas. Doesn't see all of his life coming back at him. No, no. This painting is finished.

The orchid is starting to bloom.

The cows still need to be fed. And the calves buried.

AUTHOR PROFILE

walk dog
write
trade stocks
make images
work out
work in
walk dog
write

tetonwolf.com

Made in the USA
San Bernardino, CA
26 October 2014